I0640607

Conway Edward Cartwright

Life and Letters of the Late Hon. Richard Cartwright

Conway Edward Cartwright

Life and Letters of the Late Hon. Richard Cartwright

ISBN/EAN: 9783337114220

Printed in Europe, USA, Canada, Australia, Japan

Cover: Foto ©Raphael Reischuk / pixelio.de

More available books at **www.hansebooks.com**

OF THE LATE

HON. RICHARD CARTWRIGHT,

MEMBER OF LEGISLATIVE COUNCIL IN THE FIRST PARLIAMENT
OF UPPER CANADA.

EDITED BY REV. C. E. CARTWRIGHT.

BORN 1759, DIED 1815.

> "A man with head, heart, hand
> Like one of the simple great ones gone,
>   Forever and ever by,
> Whatever they call him what care I,
> Aristocrat, Autocrat, Democrat, one
>   Who can rule, and dare not lie."
>
> TENNYSON.

TORONTO, CANADA : SYDNEY, N.S.W.:

BELFORD BROTHERS:

MDCCCLXXVI.

PRINTED AND BOUND
BY
HUNTER, ROSE AND CO.,
TORONTO.

CONTENTS.

PREFACE.

In presenting the following letters and papers to the public, I have been influenced by the idea that they might prove of considerable value to any one who was desirous of presenting to the world a true picture of the political or social history of Canada.

For the nature and variety of the subjects treated of in these pages the reader is referred to the table of contents, which include a good deal of information not easily obtainable, on war, trade, revenue, politics, &c., supplying a tolerably vivid picture of the early days of Ontario, in the words of one of the earliest settlers and most intelligent men of the time.

A short sketch of his life, taken from the funeral sermon preached by the late Bishop of Toronto, is added to the paper.

C. E. C.

Kingston, July, 1876.

CONTENTS.

PREFACE.

LIFE.

CHAPTER I.

CHAPTER II.

CHAPTER III.

LIFE

OF

HON. RICHARD CARTWRIGHT.

ABRIDGED FROM FUNERAL SERMON

BY

REV. JOHN STRACHAN.

BORN AT ALBANY—EDUCATION—STUDIES FOR THE CHURCH—REVOLU-
TION—JOINS QUEEN'S RANGERS—SERVES TWO CAMPAIGNS—PART-
NERSHIP WITH MR. HAMILTON*—HIS BUSINESS PRINCIPLES—MADE
JUDGE OF COMMON PLEAS—MEMBER OF LEGISLATIVE COUNCIL—
DECLINES SEAT IN EXECUTIVE COUNCIL—HIS PATRIOTISM IN WAR
OF 1812—LOSS OF HIS CHILDREN—HIS DEATH.

RICHARD CARTWRIGHT was born at Albany, in the State of
New York, then a British colony, on the 2nd of February,
1759. His father, an emigrant from England, was highly respectable, of great hospitality, and possessed of the most agreeable convivial talents. His mother, born of a loyal Dutch
family, was remarkable for her strength of mind, excellent
judgment, and tenacity of memory—gifts which descended
with increased vigour to her affectionate son. His education
commenced at a private school, and much pains were taken by
his parents to gratify that strong desire of information which

---

* This Mr. Hamilton was the father of the Hon. John Hamilton, of Kingston, Senator.

he exhibited from his earliest infancy.   He was permitted to
peruse every book which came in his way, nor was such pro-
miscuous reading found injurious to his taste, nor inimical to
his progress in useful learning; for the accuracy of his judgment soon taught him to distinguish the useful from the trifling.
So retentive was his memory, that he seldom forgot anything
that he read ; when, therefore, he removed to another school,
where the classics and higher branches of education were
taught, his industry and abilities secured to him the affection
of his teacher, who saw with admiration and delight his rapid
progress in Latin and Greek.   Indeed his retention of memory
gave him a facility in acquiring languages which has been seldom equalled.

To these attainments he added, by private study, an inti-
mate acquaintance with almost all the classical works in the
English tongue.   Arrived at an age when he was to look forward to his exertions for an honourable support, he began to
consider of a profession.   The extent of his knowledge, and
the pleasures which he had reaped from the cultivation of his
mind, had given him, as frequently happens, a distaste for mercantile pursuits.

The law was not congenial to his mind ; in that lucrative
profession there are many transactions which open rather a
sombre view of human nature.   The various apparatus necessary to secure property and reputation, rights public and
private, become a severe satire on mankind ; and as he knew
that much talent is employed in delaying justice and defending
wrong, he could not reconcile his mind to such exertions. This
did not prevent him from admiring many in this profession, nor
blind him to the great good which a lawyer of superior talents
and inflexible integrity might effect in preventing wrongs and

terminating contentions, directing the doubtful and instructing the ignorant. Possessing those qualities in a most eminent degree which constitute a great character and a virtuous man, he had no ambition to figure in public life, and after mature deliberation he turned his views to the Church. Perhaps a misfortune which had befallen him early in life assisted in leading him to this determination. A boy, in playing, struck him with a stone in his left eye, which deprived him almost entirely of its use, and turned the ball outwards, by which his countenance, otherwise remarkably fine, was somewhat deformed.

Of a parish priest, such as his imagination presented, he spoke always with enthusiasm. He considered him a person appointed to preserve among his people the spirit of vital religion, to be their moral guardian, to keep them in unity and in the constant practice of mutual love and good offices one towards another. The clergyman should be a pattern of moderation, temperance and contentment to all his parishioners; by this he will extend his influence among them, increase their felicity, and prepare them, by a living example, for securing that blessed immortality which the Gospel announces. Not that he was ignorant of the difficulties which a clergyman has to surmount in this country, from the laxity of religious principles, from the want of early impressions, and the general indifference to and total neglect of Gospel ordinances. But those difficulties, he was accustomed to say, would rather stimulate than impede the conscientious priest, who would find infinite delight in forming a congregation where there had been none before; changing darkness into light; promoting industry, sobriety and humanity among his people, and proving to them that even in this life the sincere Christian enjoys infinitely more happiness than any other man, and this in a great measure independent of transient things. Other stations might, he said, possess greater pomp and show, but he knew no social condition which united so many sources of the highest enjoyment—so many objects for gratifying those passions which lead to self-satisfaction. Animated by these sentiments, he turned his vigorous mind to a full preparation for discharging with ability and success the duties of a parish priest. He read the works of the most eminent divines; he applied himself to the study of Hebrew ; he could not bear the idea of mediocrity, and being able to read with care the New Testament in the original Greek, he was desirous of reading the Old Testament as it had been revealed. He was proceeding with his accustomed rapidity, and had even ventured upon biblical criticism, when the American Rebellion broke out, and changed the objects of his life. In love with retirement, and turning his whole attention towards a station which made peace and harmony the foundation of its exertions, he had never taken any interest in the various disputes which divided Great Britain and her colonies. But the time was now come when neutrality could no longer be maintained, and when it became necessary for him to take a side. Brought up in habitual reverence to the King and Parliament by his loyal parents, he did not hesitate a moment in making his choice. Well acquainted with the history of his country, he knew that Great Britain had been involved in two long and expensive wars to defend the colonies, and that they had contributed little or none of the expense ; he thought it but reasonable that they should give something towards remunerating the parent State for the vast burdens she had incurred. It is not probable that his early age enabled him to ascertain the degree of authority which might be rightfully exercised by the mother country over her colonies. It had always been asserted that Parliament possessed the power of binding them in all cases ; this was the opinion of the best informed ; it was recognised in many States, and admitted by the Legislatures of all the colonies, nor was it ever controverted by argument till the colonists had been taught, by the opposition in the British Parliament, the subtle distinction between acts for the regulation of commerce, and those which regulate their interior arrangements. The first opposition to the mother country originated from that republican disposition of the New England people which always submitted with reluctance to the constitutional authority of a government in which monarchy made a considerable part. Ever discontented and jealous of usurpation, they were continually at variance with their governors, and claiming exemptions and privileges which could not be granted. But, active in diffusing their sentiments through the other colonies, the spirit of dissatisfaction became at length so general as to enable them to break out in open rebellion. The various artifices made use of to deceive the people, the false news invented, the cruelties exercised on those attached to the King, did not escape the notice of our excellent friend, who was disgusted with their proceedings, and more zealous in defending the side which he had chosen. He was convinced that the rebellion originated from a restless democratic spirit, and that it gained ground only by the imbecility of the measures taken to crush it, the assistance of the Opposition in Parliament, and the treacherous conduct of the commanders employed by sea and land. Displeased with the selfish views of the disaffected, feeling no oppression from Parliament, nor greater restrictions than appeared necessary for the unity of all parts of the empire, and convinced that if any grievance existed rebellion was not the proper remedy, he maintained his loyalty. He had no interests to serve ; he sought not for power or emolument from commotions and bloodshed ; yet he was the steady friend of rational freedom, and as ready as any man to stand up in its defence.   Actuated by these principles he accompanied his parents into Canada, and for a time attended Colonel Butler, of the Queen's Rangers, as his Secretary.   In this station he had several opportunities, during two campaigns, of giving specimens of the penetration and courage which were such prominent parts of his character. After the conclusion of the war, which, by giving success to the rebels, has produced so many miseries to mankind, there appeared no prospect for him in the church ; he was therefore obliged to relinquish his favourite pursuits and to engage in a profession by no means congenial to his mind.   At the solici- tation of a near and worthy relation, he formed a connection with the Honourable Robert Hamilton, a gentleman of such varied information, engaging manners, and princely hospita- lity, as to be justly esteemed an honour to the Province.   His memory is gratefully remembered by thousands whom his magnanimous liberality rescued from famine.   The connection subsisted with great satisfaction to both parties for several years, when, on account of the extent of their business, a separation took place by mutual consent, Mr. Hamilton going to Niagara, and Mr. Cartwright remaining at Kingston ; but their mutual regard and friendship was only dissolved by death. Although Mr. Cartwright had found it necessary to relinquish his views of becoming a minister of the Gospel, yet he indulged always in a serious turn of mind and a strong predilection for the sacred character.   Often has my venerable friend, who was accustomed to address you from this sacred place, with much profit to your souls, lamented that circumstances had prevented a person of such eminent abilities from entering the Church, of which he must have become its chief ornament. The excellence of his disposition, his discrimination of character, his acquaintance with the human heart, would have made him singularly useful. That elevation of mind which accompanies high principle and extensive knowledge, while it presided over his mercantile pursuits, prevented him from strictly attending to petty gains, or from being tenacious of always obtaining what may be deemed, in common language, his just rights. He knew that justice, unless mixed with benevolence, may frequently become cruelty; and therefore he was lenient to his debtors, and notwithstanding his extensive concerns, seldom had recourse to law. Riches are not everything; they may be too dearly bought; and I may venture to say that never was he the cause of misery to any family. But, though this inflexible integrity and honourable dealing, which produced the same uniform conduct with young and old, ignorant and knowing, and which was more ready to recede than to be severe, had made him less wealthy than he would have otherwise been, he was possessed of all he desired—a liberal competence; and by his honourable conduct he gave a complete example of those liberal views and magnificent principles which have raised the character of the British merchant so high in the eyes of the world. Soon after his settlement in Kingston he was appointed Judge of the Common Pleas, the duties of which he discharged, without any emolument, in a way most honourable to himself and beneficial to the public. His patient attention to the causes before him, his inflexible impartiality, his singular penetration, and the strength of his judgment, added to the energetic firmness of his character, enabled him to perform, in a most correct manner, the duties of this important office. One of his brethren in another district used to say, with much *naïveté*, that "Mr. Cartwright was worth them all ; while we were poring and studying, he sees a thing almost intuitively, overawing us by his very manner, giving dignity to the court, and inspiring a respect for its decisions." On the bench he had no prejudice or predilection of any kind; accordingly, he was most attentive, mild and discriminating, for he aspired to no praise but that which might be given to the conscientious discharge of his duty. In performing the more humble, but various and useful duties of a magistrate, you are all witnesses of his eminence. His addresses to the grand juries at the Quarter Sessions will be long remembered for their sound principles, liberal views, and tempered dignity. In exerting himself to keep the peace, in apprehending and committing felons, and performing all the troublesome duties of this office, he was indefatigable. He did not drive away the injured who came to complain of the oppressor, nor did he attend to his private affairs in preference to theirs. Very few understand the duties of a magistrate; they are so numerous, and embrace so great a variety of objects, that the country is under great obligations to any worthy man who shall prepare himself for this office, and discharge its duties without any sinister motives of his own. No sooner were the provinces divided than he was appointed a member of the Legislative Council ; and I believe was never, during the remainder of his life, absent from a single session of Parliament except one. In a pecuniary point of view this attendance, every season for twenty-three years, was accompanied with great expense, besides the loss of time in conducting his private business. Nor was it merely while at the seat of government that he was occupied in legislation ; many an hour did he spend in collecting and preparing materials for useful laws, in order to render the Province prosperous and happy.

He was not one of those intuitive legislators who can sit down of a morning and write a law upon any whim that strikes their fancy ; such crude excrescences could only raise his contempt and indignation.   He deliberated coolly ; he collected information with care ; he weighed the words and sentences with the most scrupulous anxiety, that the meaning might be plain and simple, and that each clause should express that meaning perspicuously, and no other.   Nor was he one of those narrow-minded though well-intentioned statesmen who look for an immediate effect from their legislative labours ; he knew that, from the nature of mankind, many evils, after the law had afforded a remedy, disappeared slowly ; that there were many enactments of the most useful kind which seemed to take no effect, but which proceeded in silence, with slow but steady pace, to produce the most beneficial results.

Possessing great comprehension of thought, and the most vigorous talents, attended with a patience of research and a self-control highly advantageous, he was frequently content to give way to the less extended views of his colleagues, and to accept of an imperfect measure rather than lose it altogether. You can never, he would say, bring all into the same way of thinking ; some measures of great and lasting advantage to a State are slow in their operation, and appear to produce, for a season, no beneficial effect, which are yet in the end pregnant with the most precious advantages.   But you cannot expect in a public assembly always to transfuse your own views and sentiments into the minds of others.   Some are too ignorant to comprehend the force of your arguments ; some too lazy to attend to them ; many are blinded by prejudices, and some have already adopted the contrary side, which they are determined, at all hazards, to maintain.   If, therefore, you remain inflexible, even in the attainment of good, nothing will be accomplished; you must concede, and leave a good measure to make its own way after it has began to operate. Nor is it just that you should carry all your plans, however disinterested your intentions. Others may be equally so, though differing in opinion, and it is right that they should sometimes decide against you, even though wrong, that they may know from experience that they are in possession of liberty. To those who complained of the little interest many took in preparing for their legislative duties, and their narrow views in turning everything to their own county, or their own village, he used to say, that the great imperfection of national as well as domestic government arose from the little virtue and soundness of principle, not only in making laws, but in putting them in execution; that, instead of finding fault, it would be much better to act, and to remember that the wisest laws are of no use unless executed by virtue. Almost every statute that goes into general operation must be delegated to many different persons, judges, juries, constables, &c., who, if not governed by conscience, will abuse their discretionary power. Make a nation virtuous, and the laws will be wise and their execution sure. He looked for more good from a rational plan of education, disseminating moral and religious principles among the people, than from legislative enactments. He had been frequently offered a seat in the Executive Council, which he declined, not only from a conscientious feeling that he could not discharge its duties strictly, living at a distance from the seat of government, but also because he was convinced that he could do more good as a magistrate and legislator by not being identified with the Government, as an Executive Councillor must frequently be. Though never aspiring to popularity, his known probity had given him a degree of influence which no other man possessed. This made him anxious to guard the independence of his character from any possibility of imputation. His great ambition was to be useful to the Province, and to promote the prosperity of its inhabitants. In every situation in which he was placed, we behold the same dignity of character maintained, the same forgetfulness of self, the same elevation of principle, which, satisfied with the approbation of conscience, and future hopes, depended not upon the applause of men, but, on the contrary, sometimes exerted itself when friends and acquaintances were displeased, and even amidst frowns and menaces. It is true, that those did not continue long ; his inflexible probity shone through transient clouds, and many who had determined to find fault were left in admiration. It was in this elevated situation, long at the head of this Society, and possessing the love and esteem of good men, and the respectful homage of the wicked, that the late war found him ; for though taught from former experience to look for everything base and degrading from the faction that ruled our unhappy neighbours, yet he could hardly believe that open war would have been the consequence. Sound policy, interest and affection were in favour of peace ; much might be lost, but nothing could be gained by hostilities. When he found himself mistaken, all the enthusiasm of former times kindled in his bosom, and though sinking under domestic afflictions, his love for his country gave him new life. His patriotism during the whole war burnt with the most noble brightness. Not satisfied with the active discharge of his duties as colonel of the militia, he endeavoured by his writings to inspire every inhabitant of the colony with sentiments and reflections suitable to the dangerous situation of the country.

Writing from the heart, and with the most lively zeal, in the important cause, he contributed in an eminent degree to preserve that noble spirit of independence which enabled us to close the contest so gloriously. When our vindictive enemy threatened to drive us from the fertile fields that we had gained from the wilderness, to sever us from our parent state, to deprive us of all that gives dignity to man and renders life valuable, he was found actively employed in animating the militia to resistance, pointing out the folly of the boastings of the foe, and the certainty of their defeat. His unremitting exertions were continued long after the disease that destroyed . him had made great progress ; the strength of his body was not equal to the firmness of his soul ; but he continued till within a few weeks of his death to discharge public duties of the most important nature. Should any suppose that because he was always found on the side of the Government, and strenuous in protecting it from the machinations of secret and the attacks of open enemies, that he was not friendly to liberty, they would be much mistaken. No man ever displayed more firmness and independence than he in every situation. As a legislator, he thought always for himself, and was even somewhat jealous of his liberty. But when he differed from his colleagues, and opposed a measure desired by the Government, it was a difference arising from conviction ; it was not a factious opposition to exhibit his power and gain popularity ; nor did he ever allow a spirit of insolence and contradiction to thwart any measure in agitation.

His opposition was therefore equally honourable as his support, and such was the conviction of his pure integrity that it extended his influence, and, consequently, his usefulness. Always a supporter of the liberty and independence of the subject, and a steady asserter of all those privileges which every Briton enjoys by our happy constitution, he knew how easily they were reconciled to the firmest loyalty and patriotism. It was at this time that his situation appeared to combine everything that was desirable upon earth. Possessing a rare combination of excellent qualities, the most inflexible integrity, and the fairest reputation, derived from a long and uninterrupted course of steady and meritorious conduct, I could not help mentioning to him that he derived even in this life the most grateful rewards of virtue, the esteem, the love, and the veneration, not only of those who were intimately connected with him in the bonds of friendship and kindred, but of all who were witnesses of his actions and capable of appreciating the motives which produced them. In his memorable reply, he says : " This day closes my fifty-second year, and I can, I think, safely say that I have lived as much and almost as happily as anybody in the same time. What Providence may prepare for me in the remainder of my course it is impossible to foresee, but I shall always have the consolation that hitherto my life has not been idly or uselessly spent."

Enjoying so much domestic comfort, and that singleness of mind which accompanies the consciousness of well-doing, it seems that such a state was too happy for man, and by one of those mysterious decrees of Providence which astonish and confound human calculations, he was doomed to suffer the most severe calamities that could be inflicted ; the blows of adversity were aimed at his heart. That cheerful and promising family, in the bosom of which he saw rising the most engaging virtues, and from which he anticipated great happiness, was doomed to wither away before him. He was to mark the slow but certain progress of death prevailing over lives that

were dearer to him than his own. First, his second son left a
blank in this house of domestic felicity, and his death was
accompanied with circumstances that give it an interest which
cannot fail to engage the warmest sympathy of every feeling
heart. It was the reaction of virtuous principles warring
against a degrading habit, which had prevailed over his good
dispositions at a time when he was not under the eye of
parental restraint. The grief, the agitation of contending
passions, and the firm determination never again to deviate
from the true path, was too much for his physical power to
sustain. The conflict threw him into a decline, life ebbed
slowly away, but virtue continued to triumph. It was this
victory over temptation, which had been accustomed to prevail,
though purchased with his life, that rendered his death so
bitter to his affectionate father ; his sorrow was the more deep
and heartfelt, as it must be concealed from a censorious and
unfeeling world.

From this severe blow he might have returned to the world;
for while he lamented the loss of a son who displayed in his
last moments a firmness of soul capable of raising his character
to the highest rank in human excellence, he had still many
children of the fairest promise.   But, alas ! his first-born was at
that very time slowly sinking under a decline, with little or
no hopes of a recovery. 1 am sure I may with confidence appeal to all who knew this amiable young man, whether they
ever saw one so universally beloved ; the most affectionate of
sons, the kindest of brothers, joining to the strictest moral and
religious principles a heart expanding to every benevolent
thought, with a temper of uncommon sweetness : his understanding was clear, and his views noble. Never did a more excellent young man claim the sympathy of his friends. Social,

cheerful and affectionate, he was loved by those who knew him almost to enthusiasm, for his cheerfulness, arising from a mind at peace within itself, never failed to enliven his friends and make them happy. Uniformly good-humoured, easy in his conversation, of purity of disposition never surpassed, and of habitual piety, he had been for some years the most pleasant and instructive companion that his father ever enjoyed. Judge then of his feelings, and of the bitter tears he shed over him, when the hand of a relentless disease was leading him to the grave. He could not behold the brightest of his sublunary hopes vanishing away without unutterable anguish; the prop of his declining years, the protector of the family to whom they might have applied with confidence as their kind and faithful guardian, when from the course of nature his own head should be laid low. From this terrible calamity he never recovered entirely. The consolations of religion were his, but the fondest hopes of his heart were blasted; and although resigned, the world had lost its charms. His grief undermined his health; food was loathsome; he became too abstemious, and laid the foundation of that afflicting disorder which brought him to the grave. His declining health appeared for a time rather a source of joy than of sorrow, and while employed in his usual avocations, nothing appeared capable of interesting his heart, till a new calamity taught him that he had still duties to perform, and, rousing anew his tender affections, seemed to give him new life and energy, and again to awaken in him a wish to live. His eldest daughter was seized with a cruel disorder which threatened her speedy dissolution. All the tender feelings of the father were again called into action; every exertion was made for her recovery, and for a time with success, but it was only a transient return to health. The remedies given for her recovery undermined a constitution naturally delicate, and while they cured one disorder, laid the foundation of another still more fatal. He had the misery to behold his amiable and affectionate child put to death by a disorder at once painful and lingering. In her departure was seen, in the strongest light, the peculiar blessings of a peaceful end. But, alas! her parents were overwhelmed by this new and terrible calamity; they were deprived of a diamond that gladdened their hearts, and possessing all those excellencies of beauty and mind which they could desire. Her figure was elegant, her action graceful; the timid modesty of her countenance showed the ingenuousness of her soul. Her disposition was so friendly, humane, and gentle, that it was impossible to know and not to love her. Above all, she had a well-grounded assurance of the truth of Christianity, which smoothed her path to the grave. Endowed with uncommon sweetness of temper, her premature death filled this place with deep concern. All sighed at the departure of a person so richly gifted with every requisite to make her lovely; no wonder that her parents severely felt her loss. A model of filial piety, she spoke not of the progress of her disease lest she should give her parents uneasiness, and suffered without a murmur the most excruciating pain. It was at this period that she displayed that Christian patience and fortitude which resulted from deep reflection and habitual devotion, and which not only strengthened the gentle qualities of her nature, but enabled her to submit with meek resignation to the Divine will. "It has pleased Heaven," says her heartbroken father, "to take from me those who knew me best and loved me most—those whom parental affection mellowed into the tenderest friendship had entwined most closely around my heart. I, however, claim no exemption from the calamities of life, and pretend not to murmur at the dispensations of Providence ; but the wounds made by this revulsion will bleed. Where can I expect another James and another Hannah on this side of the grave ? the sources of our most delightful anticipations, the ornament and pride of our house." And again he observes : " Young was James in years, but mature in virtue. Since he was capable of reflection, he never gave, by his conduct, a moment's pain to his parents, and the only consolation they can have for his loss is the hope that their surviving children will imitate his example." And he observes of Hannah, " If ever child repaid a parent's care or merited their fondest love, it was her. Beautiful, kind, unassuming, unaffected, she was adored and beloved by all her acquaintance, and almost doated on by her parents." The progress of the war threw upon Mr. Cartwright so many duties that we thought his mind would be so much occupied as in time to divert his grief ; he ceased indeed to complain, but his constitution was impaired and his heart was broken. With that dignity and firmness which were the basis of his character, he seemed to a stranger to have recovered from his misfortunes, but the wounds which they inflicted never ceased to bleed. Never did he omit a particle of his duty ; by night and day he was ready, with his pen and sword, to defend this happy Province ; and his incessant application to business undoubtedly aggravated his disorder. A fresh calamity was threatening him : his fourth son, the most promising in point of intellectual talents of all, fell into a consumption. " It pleased God," says this excellent man, " to take to himself my dear Stephen ; and though I had long expected this termination of his disorder, I was not the less affected by it when it did arrive. Our children seem to entwine themselves about our affections in proportion to their helpless-

B

ness, and he was withal so patient and considerate, that the
separation was like tearing my heart-strings asunder. When I
compare the present state of my family with what it was but
three short years ago, I am ready to sink under those repeated
visitations which have destroyed my fairest prospects of earthly
happiness."

Little more than a year intervened between Stephen's death
and his own, yet during that period he shrunk not from business. He attended his duties in the Legislature, he assisted at
the Board of Claims, and while scarcely able to articulate or to
swallow food sufficient to support him, he continued to perform the most important functions. At length the progress of
his disorder threatened his immediate dissolution. He was
prepared to die, but always alive to the claims of his family.
He was willing to try every means to continue a little longer
among them. With this intention he went to Kamouraska to
bathe in the sea; this aggravated the symptoms, and on his return he died in Montreal. To strangers, Mr. Cartwright was
distant and reserved; there appeared even a coldness in his
manner at your first approach; but this vanished by degrees,
and his conversation was unrivalled in its power of varied
amusement, in rich display of original observations, and facility
of quotation from the best classical authors, English and Latin.
His opinion on literary productions was exceedingly correct,
for he was an excellent judge of style, and his acute discern-
ment easily detected a fallacy in reasoning. He loved poetry,
and was extremely sensible to its charms; he had even culti-
vated a poetical turn, which he possessed from nature, to a considerable extent. He relished in a high degree all our best
classical poems, and there was hardly a passage of excellence in
Shakespeare, Milton, Dryden, Pope, Thomson and Goldsmith,

or any other celebrated poet, that he could not repeat. In
social discussion he possessed powers of no common stamp,
combining accuracy of science with precision of method and
richness of illustration. His character was bold, energetic and
firm. Seldom do we find such a combination of eminent talents,
such extensive knowledge, added to so fine and excursive an
imagination. Possessing an innate love of justice and abhorrence of iniquity, he enforced upon all occasions the strictest
integrity. An enemy to affectation and insincerity, he despised
intrigue of every kind, or what in modern language is termed
address. From the steadiness of his character, it naturally
followed that he was constant in his attachments. Never did
he desert any of his friends, whom, after trial and selection, he
had pressed to his heart. Enjoying his invaluable friendship
without interruption from our first acquaintance, I feel his loss
as that of an elder brother; my wisest counsellor and surest
protector, to whom I could always apply for instruction and
consolation. With the warmest affection for his friends, he
joined an eagerness to do them good which no difficulties could
diminish ; is it then to be wondered though he carried to the
grave their love and veneration ? In their bosoms his memory
will be cherished while their hearts beat and their souls are
capable of reflection. His strict probity and inviolable love of
truth gave him an influence in the country which no other
person ever attained. Never did any man court popular applause
less, and never was any person so much esteemed by the general
voice of the Province ; it was a homage paid to virtue. Those
virtues throw a lustre over his character, and it was the study
of his life to transmit so precious an inheritance to his children.
To accomplish this most important object, and to give them a
proper foundation, he laboured unceasingly to inculcate the

principles of our holy religion upon their hearts, which he justly deemed the root of all true virtue. His was a practical religion, transfused into his life and governing his actions; not only directing his intercourse with the world, and penetrating the retirement of the closet, but entering the secret recesses of the heart. He was aware of his situation long before his death, but not a murmur escaped him; no repinings, no forgetfulness; all was peace and composure, and a steady resignation to the will of God.

His anxiety was only for his family and his friends; for himself he was ready, nay, joyful, as going from a world of pain and suffering to another of infinite happiness and duration. In a letter addressed to his friend, but not to be opened till after his decease, he says : "My infirmities are increasing so fast upon me that it would be infatuation in me to expect to live long, and I may very possibly be called away in a few days. To me this is no otherwise an object of anxiety than as it may affect my family. Adieu, my dear friend; before this reaches you I shall have finished my earthly career, which has been shortened by the afflicting events which have in the three last years prostrated my fairest hopes. I shall, without dismay, resign my soul into the hands of its Creator, trusting to the merits of our Saviour for all the blessings which Christianity offers to her friends."

LIFE AND LETTERS

OF

RICHARD CARTWRIGHT.

CHAPTER I.

EXPEDITION TO WYOMING—SO-CALLED MASSACRE A FIGHT—BRANT
DESTROYS GERMAN FLATS—BUTLER DESTROYS CHERRY VALLEY
—CANNIBALISM—GOV. HAMILTON CAPTURED BY AMERICANS AND
PUT IN IRONS—AMERICANS BURN ONONDAGO—CAPTAIN M'DON-
ELL LAYS WASTE THE SHAMOKIN SETTLEMENTS—BRANT DEFEATS
COL. FLURSTIN—GEN. SULLIVAN'S CAMPAIGN—RANGERS DEFEAT-
ED—LAY AMBUSCADE—IT FAILS—BUTLER RETREATS TO NIAGARA—
MINOR OPERATIONS.

MEMORANDUM OF INDIAN OPERATIONS FROM 1778 TO 1780,
MADE AT NIAGARA IN 1780.

AFTER the loss of many of their principal Chiefs near Fort
Stanwix, the Indians, ever eager for revenge, were easily prevailed upon to continue their hostilities against the rebels, in
which they had at first engaged with a great deal of reluctance.

It was, however, thought most prudent that they should continue quiet during the winter, and begin their depredations
on the frontier early in the spring. In consequence of this
resolution, the principal of the Six Nation Chiefs and a number
of others came to Niagara early in the season, who, after receiving very liberal presents, marched from thence on the 1st of

May with Major Butler and the Rangers, having the fertile settlement of Wyoming, a frontier of Pennsylvania, for the object
of their expedition.

That tardiness which usually attends all their operations
kept them inactive for more than a month ; a great part of this
time was spent in deliberations, in which some adherents of
the rebels frequently occasioned much perplexity, and it cost
Major Butler some pains to prevent the other Indians from
being diverted by them from their purpose.   They, however, at
length determined to proceed, and on the 1st of July entered
the settlement, the party consisting in the whole of 464 Indians and 110 Rangers. That day and the next, two small forts,
in which were a number of women and children and a few men,
surrendered on condition of having their lives spared and being allowed to retire into the country.   The Indians at first,
seeing the inhabitants shut up in forts, and in some measure
secured from their fury, thought of nothing but of scattering
through the settlement to vent it upon the cattle and buildings,
and at the same time to collect as much plunder as they could.
Major Butler, however, by his earnest entreaty, prevailed upon
them to keep in a body till he tried what effect a flag of truce
would have, and finding it attended with such unexpected success in the two first instances, they were desirous of getting
possession of all the rest of the forts by the same method, and
a flag was accordingly sent to the principal fort on the 3rd ;
but was insulted, and soon after the greatest part of that garrison, and some small ones below it, in all about 450 men, commanded by a Colonel Butler, came out to attack them, on
which a very warm engagement ensued, and lasted for about
fifteen minutes, when the rebels retreated with precipitation,
and were hotly pursued by the Indians, who took 226 scalps

and three prisoners, and several were besides drowned in attempting to pass the river.

Major Butler's loss was only seven wounded, two of whom died of their wounds. This victory made them entire masters of all the settlement, as it occasioned such a panic that all the forts were either abandoned or surrendered, on the same conditions as the two first, before the 7th instant. Most of the houses were burnt except such as belonged to people under the name of Loyalists ; a very large number of cattle were driven off ; and effects to a great amount brought away in plunder by the Indians.

All this was said to be done without any acts of cruelty being committed by the savages ; for the deliberate murder of prisoners after they are brought into their camp is not, it seems, reckoned among acts of cruelty by these barbarous wretches. On the 10th, Major Butler arrived at Tioga, and on the 14th set out for Niagara with a party of the Rangers and several families of Loyalists; having previously detached Captain Caldwell, with part of the Rangers and also some of the Indian officers, to Aughquaga to assist Captain Brant, and at the same time engage recruits for the corps of Rangers from the people who were at that time flocking in from different parts of the frontiers to avoid serving in the militia. Captain Brant had gone from Niagara in April, destroyed the settlement of Cobuskill, in the upper part of Tryon County, and some other settlements in its neighbourhood, and was keeping that part of the country in a constant alarm, when hearing that the rebels intended to send a force into the Indian country, he retired to Aughquaga, where Captain Caldwell joined him, and they continued some time under continual apprehensions of being attacked. He had requested the Senecas to come to his assistance and join in his operations ; but through some jealousies and animosities which now began to break out, they refused. About this time Captain Tire, with a party of Mohawks, arrived at Niagara, and proceeded to Aughquaga.

Towards the latter end of September, their alarms being pretty well quieted, Captain Brant prevailed on his coadjutors, not without some difficulty, to go against the German Flats, which they destroyed without meeting any opposition, and drove off a great number of cattle, but the inhabitants had all taken shelter in the fort. Captain Butler, going into the Indian country at this time with a party of Rangers, was, agreeable to orders, joined by Captain Caldwell and his detachment at Tioga ; Captain Tire returned immediately to Canada ; and Captain Brant, with his volunteers and only seven or eight Indians, went down towards the Minisink, where he burnt a number of houses and barns, destroyed a large quantity of grain, and did much other mischief. While this was doing, a party of riflemen burnt the village of Aughquaga, and about the middle of October a Colonel Hartley with a number of men came up the river from Wyoming, and put the camp above Tioga into a good deal of consternation ; but being himself frightened by the appearance of a force he did not expect, he, without doing much mischief, retreated hastily back to Wyoming, which the rebels had again taken possession of in force soon after Major Butler left it. About the 1st of November Captain Butler, being joined by a number of Seneca and other Indians, and also by Captain Brant, marched against Cherry Valley, which they reached on the 11th. This settlement was soon destroyed, a number of the inhabitants and some officers and soldiers, who happened to be out of the fort, killed and taken, and such acts of wanton cruelty committed by the blood-thirsty savages as humanity would shudder to mention.

These are the principal Indian operations in this quarter for 1778, but a number of small parties were constantly going to and from different parts of the frontier, and excited such a general terror that the inhabitants abandoned a great part of the frontier settlements entirely. In the autumn of 1788, about 1,500 men, including militia, were sent by the rebels to Fort Pitt, under the command of a Colonel Gibson, in order to secure the frontiers of Pennsylvania, and intimidate and bring to terms the Indians in that quarter, to do which the more effectually it was thought proper to send forward a part of these forces to build a fort at the Tuskarawas, but this by no means had the desired effect. The Indians were continually hovering about this post, and not a man could stir out of it without falling into their hands, so that they at last abandoned it early in the summer of 1779.

In the course of the winter, one Davis or Mesuray, and a German doctor, with some soldiers, left Fort Pitt, intending to come to Niagara, but having consumed all their provisions, and destitute of the hope of a further supply, some of the soldiers attempted to return ; four, however, remained behind besides Davis and the doctor, two of whom soon died with cold and hunger, and the other two, eating very ravenously of the flesh of their comrades, expired immediately after the horrid meal ; and the other two survivors, both deprived of the use of their limbs by the frost, were left under the cruel alternative of either starving or subsisting on the carcases of their late companions. The latter, however hard, was, of course, their choice, and they dragged on their existence in this miserable manner for several weeks, when they were found by a party of Indians, in the month of February, with some of the human flesh about them, and brought to Niagara.

In order to cover the frontiers of Virginia, and bring, if possible, the Western Indians over to the rebel side, Colonel Clarke, with a number of picked men, set out from the back parts of that Province in the summer of 1778, took possession of the Illinois, where he found a number of friends in the French inhabitants of the place, and it was apprehended that he might advance still further, and by his success draw over the Indians, and finally endanger Detroit itself. Governor Hamilton, to prevent these bad consequences, and from some other motives of a private nature, which made him wish to leave Detroit, set out in the fall with a very few soldiers, La Motte's company of volunteers, some militia and a number of Indians, and took possession of Port St. Vincent without opposition, though the inhabitants had before declared in favour of Clarke. In this place he remained till the beginning of March, 1779, in great security, when Clarke came upon him by surprise, and the Governor was under the necessity of surrendering himself and party as prisoners of war, and was sent into the interior part of the country, where he has ever since remained shut up in prison and loaded with irons. This disaster occasioned a great alarm at Detroit, and Captain Lemoult, the commanding officer there at that time, immediately set about building a strong though small fort on a commanding ground for the better security of the place, and a company of Rangers was sent from Niagara to reinforce his garrison. During all the winter the rebels had been making depots of provisions on the frontiers, and every other preparation for a western expedition, the object of which was thought to be Detroit both by the Commander-in-Chief and General

Haldimand—and consequently every precaution was taken to secure that place—while the parts against which it was really intended were left in a manner unguarded. The Indians of the Six Nations, after the close of their campaign, if it may be so called, came in crowds to Niagara to receive the presents intended for them, and indulge their passion for liquor, in both of which they were liberally gratified. At the same time several councils were held with the chiefs, wherein every argument was used to make them persevere in the active part they had taken, and promises of support given to encourage them ; and they were exhorted in the meanwhile, as being a matter of consequence, to keep a strict watch upon all the motions of the enemy along the frontiers.

Some months elapsed in transactions of this kind, and the Indians had scarcely returned to their villages when they were all thrown into the greatest consternation by the destruction of Onondago, which was burnt by a party of the rebels about the 20th of April, 1779, and several of the Indians carried off as prisoners. Messengers were hourly coming in from the Indians, whose fears had multiplied 600 men to 6,000, requesting immediate assistance, and reproaching Colonel Bolton with having abandoned them to the resentment of people whom they had made their enemies merely on our account and at our most earnest solicitations. Colonel Bolton resolved upon sending them immediately such succour as he was able. Major Butler accordingly set out to their assistance on the 1st of May with about 200 men, including Rangers, and a small detachment of the 8th Regiment, and the officers, &c., of the Indian Department. Part of this force was sent by water to Irondequot with provisions. This alarm soon blew over, as the rebels retired immediately, having at that time had nothing

further in view than to destroy the Onondago village, which
lay nearest to them, and get some prisoners into their hands
that might serve as hostages at least for that nation. However, it was thought best that this small force should continue
in the Indian country, to be ready to oppose any other attempts
that the rebels might make that way, and the village of Onondago was judged the most proper place of rendezvous for that purpose.   While here, Major Butler received letters from General
Haldimand enclosing a speech to the Six Nations and Con-
federates, promising them that he would send Sir John Johnson and a number of men early in the summer to take post at
Oswego, which was what the Indians had very much at heart,
and had several times requested to have done.   He also sent
a menacing speech to the Oneidas, and deputies from the different nations of Canada and some of the western nations, at
his request, to hold a meeting with them, and endeavour by
persuasions and threats to draw them off from the rebels ; but
to no purpose, as the Oneidas refused to meet them except at
their own village, whither it was not thought prudent to let
them go. They therefore returned again to Canada, and one of
the principal chiefs of the Six Nations was sent with them, in
the name of the whole Confederacy, to urge the General on the
subject of taking post at Oswego.   While these deputies were
in the country of the Six Nations, they, in conjunction with
them, addressed a very spirited speech to the western Indians,
who, it was apprehended, were at that time wavering, which
was said to have had a very good effect.   The want of provisions,
which was in a great measure irremediable, made it impossible
for Major Butler to attempt anything material; however, it
was resolved at all events to send a party into the country, in
order, if possible, to procure some cattle to subsist upon ; and,

accordingly, fifty Rangers, under the command of Captain Mc-
Donell, were sent off on the 9th of July to the west branch of
the Susquehanna, and were joined on their way by about 120
Indians.

They came upon the settlements near the Shamokin on the
27th, and the next day they took a small fort called Fort Free-
land, which was defended by thirty men, who surrendered on
promise of being sent prisoners to Niagara, and that their women and children, of which there were many in the fort,
should be allowed to retire into the country, which was punc-
tually fulfilled.   The same day he defeated a party of about
eighty rebels that came to attack him, killing the captain and
between thirty and forty privates, with the loss of only one
Indian killed; and, after having burnt thirty miles of a close-
settled country, which the inhabitants in general had abandoned at his approach, and driven off 116 head of cattle (many of
which the Indians afterwards stole), he returned on the 10th
of August with part of the cattle, affording a very seasonable
relief.   Captain Brant also, who came into the Indian country
the latter end of June, collected together a party of Indians,
with whom and some of his volunteers he went towards the
Minisink, but found the people of that settlement so well upon
their guard that he could do nothing more than burn a few
houses.   On his retreat he was attacked by a party of the
militia, under the command of Colonel Flurstin, whom he defeated with the loss of their colonel and many others; the loss
on his side was four or five killed, and ten or twelve wounded,
some of whom afterwards died of their wounds.   In the meantime the rebels were assembling a large body of troops at Wyoming and Lake Otsego, and, having everything in readiness by
the beginning of August, began their march and appeared at

Tioga on the 9th of that month, but a day or two after Captain McDonell had left it, and before it was known that they were even in motion.

They immediately began to build a fort, and on the 14th a large party of them advancing burnt Shimong, and were proceeding further when they were waylaid by some Delawares, who killed and wounded several of them, but were obliged to retreat leaving one man dead on the field. The rebels, however, thought proper to advance no further for the present, but returned in some haste to Tioga, and applied themselves with great industry to complete their fort. On the first notice of the appearance of the enemy, runners were sent off to all the villages to alarm the Indians and hurry them as fast as possible to Canadasago, the place of general rendezvous ; an express was also dispatched to Captain Butler, who, with such of the Rangers as had not gone with Captain McDonell, was removed to the mouth of the Genesea River for the convenience of being supplied with provisions ; he arrived on the 15th, as did also a great part of the Indians the same afternoon. The next day being taken up in performing the ceremonies of the war feast and war dance, on the 17th the whole, amounting to between 400 and 500 marched from Canadasago, and on the 22nd encamped at Chuchnut, or New Town, twelve miles distant from the enemy. Captain Brant and party, who were lying here, and the Delawares and others in the neighbourhood, increased the force that was to oppose the rebels to about 700 men. Every endeavour of the Indians and Rangers to get a prisoner or obtain any certain information of their number was ineffectual ; however, it was found that they had pushed a considerable part of their force to Oswego, a place sixteen miles east of Tioga, with the design, as was supposed, to facilitate their junction with the troops under General Clinton, who were to come from Lake Otsego. This they effected without any interruption. On the 27th, Major Butler was informed that the enemy were on their march towards him, and as the Indians had determined to make one general attempt to stop their progress, he, in concert with them, took possession of a rising ground about a mile from the camp at Chuchnut, and threw up a slight breastwork of logs, which was covered with bushes, the whole better calculated to conceal his men than to protect them from the fire of the enemy. Here he waited the coming of the enemy, who made their appearance early in the afternoon of the 29th. They were commanded by General Sullivan, who, having discovered the situation of Major Butler and the Indians, sent some riflemen to amuse them at long shot while he made dispositions for a general attack. He sent two brigades, commanded by Clinton and Poor, to encompass a mountain that lay to the left of Major Butler's lines, in order to gain his rear ; and another along the bank of the Cayoga River, which lay to his right, to attack him on that side ; while under cover of the wood he placed his artillery, consisting of four small pieces of cannon, a royal and a howitzer, in front, where he had also posted the riflemen, and kept a brigade commanded by a General Maxwell as a reserve. As soon as he supposed the troops to the right and left had reached their appointed stations he ordered his artillery to fire, which they did in so good a direction that many of the Indians fled immediately, and in a few minutes Major Butler was obliged to make a general retreat. The greater part took to the mountain, where the enemy had got before them, and maintained a kind of running fight along the side of it ; keeping the rebels at bay for a considerable time, till at length finding themselves on the point of being surrounded, every man made the best of his way to escape as he could. Many of the Indians never stopped till they reached their own villages, and took away in their flight several of the baggage horses that had been sent forward some miles to be out of the way in case of accidents. Major Butler halted at the Nanticoke Town, a village five miles distant from the place of action, till evening, and proceeded, with such of the Rangers and Indians as he could then collect, five miles further and then halted till the morning. In the night Captain Butler, with several other officers and about forty men, who it was feared were lost, joined him, and upon strict inquiry it was found that there were only four Rangers and five Indians killed and taken, and three Rangers and nine Indians wounded. General Sullivan, by too great haste in firing his artillery, in a manner forced his prey out of his hands; for had he delayed this till Clinton and Poor got around the mountain, it would have been impossible for Major Butler and party to have escaped, and they all must have inevitably been either killed or taken. The Indians were so intimidated by this defeat that they could not be brought again to face the enemy, and Major Butler was obliged to retreat as the rebels continued to advance, which they did so rapidly that on the 11th of September they reached Candargo. Major Butler, with the Rangers and part of the Indians, was then at Canawagoras, where they arrived on the 9th, and the rest of the Indians that had not fled to Niagara were at Genesea, about nine miles distant, but so dispirited that they could hardly be got to send small scouts to observe the motions of the enemy. Major Butler had written to Colonel Bolton an account of what had happened as soon as he was able, which was not till the 1st of September. He here received an answer from him, acquainting him that he had sent the Light Infantry Company of the 8th by water, with orders to land at the Genesea River, and join him immediately and that the Light Company of the 34th, and emigrants who were hourly expected at Niagara, should follow them as soon as possible.   The Indians, who, at Major Butler's instance, had agreed once more to face the rebels, began to recover their spirits at this intelligence ; and that they might not have time to relapse into their former despondency, Captain McDonell was immediately despatched to the mouth of the Genesea River to bring up the reinforcements with all expedition. But before this could be done the enemy drew so near that Major Butler, with the Rangers and Indians, only in all about 350, was obliged to march with all expedition to the place chosen for an ambuscade, to prevent the rebels getting there before him.   This spot was about the side of a hill opposite to the Village of Conighsas, at the foot of which was a deep morass extending far to the right, and a lake to the left, and the path through which the rebels must of necessity pass wound along the hill that the Rangers and Indians were to take possession of. Major Butler reached this on the 13th, in the morning, and found the rebels employed very busily in making a bridge over the morass.

His small force was posted to the best advantage, and lay till about noon, expecting the rebels to advance, when they were alarmed by a firing in their rear at the right of the line, on which the whole moved to that quarter, those to the left making a circuit to get beyond where it was imagined, from the firing, the rebels had begun an attack.   In a few minutes it was discovered that it was only a rebel scout of 26 men that had been sent the night before to Genesea, and on its return had fallen in with the right of the Rangers and Indians,

O

that had occasioned this alarm. The whole of this party were killed except a lieutenant and one private, who were taken prisoners, and one or two others who made their escape. The lieutenant stated that the army under General Sullivan consisted of between 4,000 and 5,000 men, and that they intended to advance no farther than Genesea. This information and a certainty of being discovered made it necessary for Major Butler, without loss of time, to retreat, and crossing the Genesea River he remained at the Genesea Village that night, the rebels being encamped about three miles off, on the opposite side of the river, which it was at that time difficult to pass. The two prisoners were stripped and beaten, and treated with every kind of indignity by the Indians ; and when at last they were given in care of a guard of Rangers, and sent before the rest to Genesea, as soon as they entered that village, in spite of what the guard could do, they were immediately tomahawked by some Indians who had been afraid to venture out, and their bodies treated in too indecent a manner to be described. This, however, was no more than a just retaliation ; the party the lieutenant commanded had the night before killed an Indian at Coshequa, a village three miles from Genesea, and exercised the most shocking and scandalous indignities on his dead body. Early on the morning of the 14th Major Butler quitted Genesea to make the best of his way to Niagara, and marched that day near 30 miles. The next morning he was joined by the detachment of the 8th, who, from the route they came, must have barely escaped falling in with the rebels ; the detachment of the 34th and the emigrants met him soon after, having marched from Niagara by land.

Some thoughts were then entertained of turning back, but as there was no prospect of effecting anything against such superior numbers, and his provisions of every kind being nearly expended, Major Butler determined to proceed to Niagara, where he arrived on the 18th with the troops, Rangers, and a swarm of Indians. General Sullivan entered Genesea, the last of the Indian towns towards Niagara, on the 14th, soon after Major Butler left it, which was the eighteenth day from the time of his leaving Tioga. After burning the town and destroying the corn, he returned to Tioga with all expedition, and without the smallest interruption, and having demolished the fort he had built there, hastened to join General Washington. A part of his army returned by the way of Fort Stanwix, and destroyed Skaias, Cayouga, and such other villages as lay in their route. While the country of the Six Nations was thus overrun on this side, the Delawares and Upper Senecas settled in the neighbourhood of Presque Isle, and lower down towards the Ohio, were invaded with the same success. As soon as the General was informed of the progress of the rebels, he sent off Sir John Johnson with the greater part of his own and the 34th Regiment, and a company of German Chasseurs, and Captain Fraser with the Canada Indians; and Colonel Johnson came also at the same time to the assistance of the Six Nations; but the mischief was done, and the rebels had retreated before they reached Carleton Island. On receiving this intelligence, Sir John determined to convey his troops to Great Asserotus, where he requested Major Butler to join him with the Indians and Rangers, and bring with him all the horses he could collect, intending from thence to march by the shortest route to attack the fort, which was supposed to be still kept at Tioga.

With this design he left Carleton Island; but being obliged by the wind to make sail for Niagara, he was there soon convinced of the impossibility of putting his plan in execution. However, as soon as the Oneidas had taken an active part in the rebel invasion, it was thought that the other Indians would readily concur in an enterprise against them, which was accordingly resolved on ; and about 150 Rangers being added to his force, he, accompanied by Colonel Johnson, set sail for Oswego on the 10th of October, and landed the troops on the 13th, at night, and Major Butler, who came along the Lake with some Indians, arrived there a few days after. Captain Brant, who conducted a party of Indians by land, did not come up as was expected, and it was found that the Indians, particularly those from Canada, were much averse to go against the Oneidas. Under these circumstances, directions came from the General to Sir John to put the troops into winter quarters, in consequence of which he quitted Oswego on the 26th October, in the evening, having occasioned a great alarm in the country and taken three Oneidas that had been reconnoitring the camp, as also a rebel sergeant from Fort Stanwix, who fell in with one of his scouts. In the course of the summer several parties of Canadian Indians had been on excursions to Mohawk River and German Flats, one of which surprised and took an officer and twenty men, near Fort Stanwix, cutting hay. In the spring Captain Bird also set out from Detroit with a large number of Indians, at their desire, to go against the rebel post at Tuskarawas ; but the Indians being rather backward, he was under a necessity of returning without doing anything material. Lieut. Bennett also, some time in the summer, went with a large party of the Western Indians from Mishilimacinac to St Joseph's, with an intention of doing something against Mr. Clarke, who continued about the country of the Illinois, but was in a manner abandoned by the Indians, and obliged to return.   In the month of October a party of Indians from Detroit, conducted by Simon Gertie, an interpreter, fell in with a party of rebels under a Colonel Rogers, going down the Ohio in boats.   They killed forty and took the Colonel, and all the boats but one fell into their hands.   Colonel Johnson, on his return from Oswego, by desire of the General, and at the instance of Colonel Bolton, endeavoured to prevail on part of the Indians to remove to Canada and Carleton Island, in order that the rest might be more conveniently supplied.

Between 500 and 600, chiefly Delawares and Onondagos, consented, not without reluctance, to go ; the rest, amounting to upwards of 3,000, exclusive of those whose villages and corn escaped, were maintained at Niagara during the winter.

At first there was much murmuring and complaining, but as every means was used to quiet them, this soon subsided, and in the month of February, 1780, several parties—and one pretty large one, conducted by Captain Brant—went out on the frontiers.

About this time the rebels, under pretence of writing to Colonel Johnson concerning an exchange of prisoners, sent four of the principal Sachems, in their interest, to endeavour to engage the Six Nations to a neutrality.   Though these on their arrival were confined in the fort, yet after some time, at the desire of the Indians, they were allowed to open their business in public, which they did, but apparently to no purpose; and in a speech delivered by Aaron, the Mohawk Chief, in reply to what they had said, they were reproached in the severest terms for their defection from the confederacy, and their servile adherence to the rebels.   Had deputies been sent to them by the rebels, while in that consternation which their first appearance and successes in the Indian country had raised, they might in all probability have brought the Indians to terms ; but it was now too late—they had no longer anything to lose, and their only care was how to be revenged for the destruction of what they held most dear. The first parties returning successful encouraged others; and so many were for going out to war, that it was found difficult to prevail on any large number of them to go and plant corn at proper places for their subsistence. In this, however, indolence might have a considerable share. Numbers of them were almost every day going to different parts of the country, in larger or smaller parties, and the rebels must have found that their grand Western Expedition, attended with such vast labour and enormous expense, instead of conquering, had only served to exasperate the Indians.

In taking a view of the Indian war, it is certain that it has very much distressed the rebels by destroying some of their best settlements, drawing off vast quantities of their cattle, and obliging them to leave the greatest part of their frontiers, from Canada to Virginia, uncultivated, besides laying them under the necessity of keeping several thousand men embodied merely to oppose the Indians.

But, besides that, the expenses of carrying it on have hitherto at least been fully adequate to these advantages. The cruelties that have attended it, and been exercised indiscriminately on friend and foe, without distinction of sex or age, when seriously considered, must make it be regarded with general abhorrence.

CHAPTER II.

LETTER TO ISAAC TODD, ESQ.—FIRST PARLIAMENT—ESTABLISHMENT OF ENGLISH LAW—CUSTOM-HOUSE BILL THROWN OUT BY UPPER HOUSE —OBJECTIONS TO THE SEAT OF GOVERNMENT ON THE TRANCKE —SECOND LETTER TO TODD—COMMISSIONERS ON REVENUE — DE- FECT OF MARRIAGE LAW — HIS DISGUST AT POLITICS—GOVERNOR SIMCOE AT YORK—HIS CANVAS HOUSE — BUILDING REGULATIONS —THIRD LETTER — INDIGNATION AT CHARGE OF DISLOYALTY — DEPRECATES ESTABLISHMENT OF ECCLESIASTICAL COURTS — AD- DRESS TO GRAND JURY — PROCEEDINGS OF THIRD SESSION — JUDICATURE BILL—LAWYERS BY ACT OF PARLIAMENT—REVENUE COMMISSIONERS — ALARM AT DETROIT — CANADIANS KILLED — LETTER TO MAJOR LOTHBRIDGE — LORD DORCHESTER'S SPEECH — SKIRMISH NEAR DETROIT—PORK CURING FOR TROOPS.

To Isaac Todd, Esq.

KINGSTON, 21st October, 1792.

DEAR SIR,—I was favoured with a letter from you by the spring ships, and am much obliged to you for the kind men- tion you were so good as to make of me to some of the officers of the new government.   The Chief Justice appears to be a very worthy and respectable man, and I am extremely sorry that his necessary attendance at head-quarters, which at present is at Navy Hall, opposite Niagara, will deprive me of the pleasure and benefit of much of his company and conversation. It is but a few days since I returned from thence, the first session of our Legislature having ended only on the 15th. Some useful regulations of police have been enacted, but

the material part of the business has been to establish the
English laws as the rule of decision in all cases of controversy
relating to property and civil rights, excluding, however, the
bankrupt and poor laws, and those relative to ecclesiastical
rights and dues, which are manifestly inapplicable to the situation of this country.   The trial by jury is also established in
all causes above forty shillings, according to the English mode ;
but it has not been thought advisable to change our Writ of
Summons, or rules of proceeding in our Courts, for the English
Capias, and the complicated, elaborate, and artificial systems of
Westminster Hall ; ' which have always appeared to me the
most fruitful sources of oppression and chicanery, and to be
rather calculated to swell the importance and fill the pockets
of the professors of the law, than for the speedy and effectual
administration of justice.   Thus far all is very well, but some
of the proceedings of the Lower House have a tendency to
show that the objections made to the division of the Province
as likely to obstruct their trade, and create separate interests
between its two portions, were better founded than I at first
thought them.   A Bill passed the House almost unanimously
for establishing custom-houses and appointing officers at the
Point of Bodet and on the Ottawa river, for the purpose of
levying a duty of sixpence per gallon on all rum and wine
that should enter the Province of Upper Canada.   Not to
mention the impolicy and inexpediency of the tax even so far
as it would operate upon the trade and consumption of the
settled parts of the country, it appeared so highly unjust
as levying a contribution upon our fellow-subjects in Lower
Canada who come to trade within our geographical limits, indeed, but far beyond the sphere of our influence, and where
we can neither protect nor facilitate their commerce, as for ex-

ample, to the North-West and Mississippi, that it met with but a single friend in the Upper House. However, these gentlemen are so full of the idea of getting money, even for county charges, without any apparent expense to themselves, that they cannot, or will not see the injustice and impropriety of the measure, and I have no doubt will renew the attempt at the next session ; not considering that if they should succeed, which is not at all probable, the Lower Province would have it in their power to retaliate upon them most severely.

The River Trancke is still talked of as the seat of government, but I hope this plan will not be persisted in, for it appears to me as complete a piece of political Quixotism as I recollect to have met with, and will be going out of the way of the inhabited part of the country, instead of coming to govern it. The maxim to follow nature not to face it is as proper for our guide in politics as in all other concerns ; and however splendid the project may be of establishing a capital that shall give laws to a numerous population which is to cover the immense peninsula formed by the lakes, and the Ottawa and St. Lawrence rivers, it is a scheme perfectly utopian, to which nature has opposed invincible obstacles ; unless Mongolfier's ingenious invention could be adapted to practical purposes, and air balloons be converted into vehicles of commerce.

To what is to be ascribed the present state of improvement and population of this country ? Certainly not to its natural advantages, but to the liberality which Government has shewn towards the Loyalists who first settled it ; to the money spent by the numerous garrisons and public departments established amongst us ; and the demand for our produce which so many unproductive consumers occasion on the spot. As long as the British Government shall think proper to hire people to come over to eat our flour, we shall go on very well, and continue to make a figure, but when once we come to export our produce, the disadvantages of our remote inland situation will operate in their full force, and the very large portion of the price of our produce that must be absorbed by the expense of transporting it to a place of exportation, and the enhanced value that the same cause must add to every article of European manufacture, will give an effectual check to the improvement of the country beyond a certain extent; the farther we go, the more powerfully must these causes operate; and when we go beyond the banks of Lake Ontario, it will cost as much to bring our rude produce to market, as it will be worth, and yet from such exports alone it is that we can become beneficial to the mother country, who certainly can have no intention to make us manufacturers. I believe, indeed, that the origin of our settlements took its rise from motives more noble than views of commercial advantages; namely, to provide a comfortable asylum for the unfortunate Loyalists reduced to poverty and driven into exile by their attachment to Britain; and it was, perhaps, necessary to crown the generous conduct which has been held with regard to them, that they should have the benefit of the English laws and form of Government. But on the present plan this object is lost sight of for an *ignis fatuus*, and the Government will " waste its sweetness on the desert air ; " the energy will be spent where it has nothing to operate upon ; and much money will be lavished away, where it can be of little permanent advantage to the Province, however useful it may be to some individuals. Whereas, had the Governor fixed his residence at this end of Lake Ontario, between which and the Point of Bodet, lies the greatest mass of our population, its influence, co-operating with the comparative advantages of the situation, would have had a powerful, beneficial, and lasting effect.   And much chagrin would have been spared to the inhabitants of the two lower districts, who compose full three-fourths of the population of the Province, and who cannot be pleased to find that they are to be neglected, and left to themselves, while Government is pursuing, at a very great expense, imaginary advantages.   I could say a great deal more on this subject, but my letter is already swelled to an immoderate length, and I should not have gone even so far, had it not been to satisfy you that my sentiments, however uncourtly, are founded in reason and truth, and do not proceed from prejudice or interested considerations.   I have given you this sketch of politics rather in compliance with your request, than from an expectation of its attracting much of your attention ; while you are so near such important scenes as are now acting on the continent of Europe ; where the worthy triumvirate of Russia, Prussia and Austria seem determined to rivet the fetters of despotism upon mankind, and show themselves equal enemies to the temperate reforms of Poland, and the extravagant republicanism of France.

To Isaac Todd, Esq.

KINGSTON, Oct. 14th, 1793·

DEAR SIR,—Your request, and the flattering reception you have given my former letter, induces me to attempt to give you some further account of the public business of the Province. The inclosed paper, containing the titles of Bills passed during the second session of our Legislature, will show that it has not been an idle one.   Some of these Acts are very well calculated for arranging the police of the country, and the one authorizing the Lieutenant-Governor to appoint Commissioners is intended as a means of amicably adjusting with the Lower Provinces every matter of revenue in which both may be concerned. So far is very well. But, as I foresaw, the Custom House Bill was again revived and again rejected, and there are so many private views blended with this measure, that it will not be easily relinquished by its partisans. For instance, now that the members of the Lower House are to have ten shillings per diem, to be paid by their respective Counties, during their attendance, the Speaker thinks he ought to have a handsome salary ; and how else is the money to be raised without exciting public clamour ? Besides, two or three appointments in this department, with a good salary annexed, would afford a very comfortable provision for some of the members; and, for so young a country, I assure you we are beginning to have a wonderful acuteness in making discoveries of this kind. The Marriage Act was necessary, and is useful as far as it goes, but it is defective in omitting to make provision for the marriages of Dissenters ; and every effort will be made at the next meeting of the Legislature to put this business on a more liberal footing. Amendments to that effect were only withdrawn in the last session on the most positive assurances that representations would be made at home relative to the propriety of relaxing in this particular. Indeed, the caution with which everything relative to the Church or Dissenters is guarded in the Act of Parliament which establishes our constitution, and the zeal and tenaciousness of the Executive Government in this country on this head, has always astonished me. When a particular system has been long adopted and acted upon, some evil may perhaps result from a change, although in its principles it may be neither liberal nor just, and at all events there is the bugbear innovation to guard the abuse ; but to make this abuse an essential principle, and where a new Government is to be formed, as in the present case, among a people composed of every religious denomination, and nineteen-twentieths of whom are of persuasions different from the Church of England, to attempt to give to that Church the same exclusive political advantages that it possesses in Great Britain, and which are even there the cause of so much clamour, appears to me to be as impolitic as it is unjust.   In the present times one would expect better things from Ministers.   That these remarks may not be imputed to prejudice, I think it necessary to mention that I am one of the small number of churchmen in the country.   For my part, I assure you I begin to be disgusted with politics.   On the division of the Province, as we had no previous establishments in our way, I fondly imagined that we were to sit down cordially together to form regulations solely for the public good ; but a little experience convinced me that these were the visions of a novice, and I found our Executive Government disposed to calculate their measures as much with a view to patronage and private endowment as the prosperity of the colony.   In this I doubt not they will be sufficiently successful, from the interested complaisance of some of our legislators, and the ignorance of more, who are incapable of foreseeing the consequences of their concessions.   But such policy is as shortsighted as it is illiberal ; and however little it may be noticed at present, if persisted in and pushed very far will unquestionably be sowing the seeds of civil discord, and perhaps laying the foundations of future revolutions.   For though almost everybody is now too much taken up with providing the means of subsistence to have leisure for canvassing public measures, yet as we advance in population and improvement they will become objects of more general attention, and in sound policy ought to be so calculated as not to furnish cause of disgust to the real patriot, or pretext for clamour to the pretended one. In the course of our proceedings I have found how completely the spirit of that part of the Act might be evaded which professes to make the Legislative Council entirely independent, by giving the members their seats for life. It is only to compose the majority of it—as has in fact been done—of Executive Councillors and officers of Government dependent for their salaries on the good pleasure of the Governor. The Governor is at present at Toronto, where he has laid out a town plot, which he has called York, and where I am told he intends to pass the winter in his canvas house, for there is yet no other built, nor preparations for any; his regiment is also to hut themselves there.

This situation for the capital unites many advantages, as it will contribute to the more speedy settling of the vacant lands on both sides of it, and be a means of sooner uniting the settlements above the Bay of Kenty and below the head of Lake Ontario, and also as it lays at the entrance of a communication into Lake Huron by Lake La Claye, which may by-and-bye be found practicable and useful. But, notwithstanding this, he does not scruple to 'say that he has his eye still fixed on the River Trancke; and though he may for awhile put up with the Town of York and the River Humber, he seems to be satisfied with nothing less than another Thames and a second London. You will smile perhaps when I tell you that even at York a town lot is to be granted in the front street only on condition that you shall build a house of not less than forty-seven feet front, two stories high, and after a certain order of architecture. In the second street they may be somewhat less in front, but the two stories and the mode of architecture are indispensable;

and it is only in the back streets and alleys that the tinkers
and tailors will be allowed to consult their taste and circumstances in the structure of their habitations, upon lots of one-
tenth of an acre. Seriously, our good Governor is a little wild
in his projects, and seems to imagine that he can in two or three
years put the country into a situation that it is impossible it
can arrive at in a century; and I fear that a great deal of expense will by this means be thrown away, which, under the
management of a less sanguine temper, would have been productive of solid benefit to the colony. For example, how useful might the Rangers have been, had they been employed in
the service for which they were ostensibly raised, of opening
roads and building bridges between the different settled parts
of the country ; but this is a business that the inhabitants are
left to do of themselves as well as they can, and the only piece
of work of this kind that these folks, who were " to level moun-
tains and make valleys rise," have been employed in at all, is
in cutting a road from the head of Lake Ontario to the River
Trancke, where there is yet not a single inhabitant, and in
this duty there is at present a captain and one hundred men
engaged. But while I am thus free in my strictures, I must
also say that the Governor merits very great praise for his indefatigable industry in exploring in person the communication
between the different parts of the country. Last winter he
went to Detroit on snow shoes ; early this spring he coasted the
Lake from Niagara to Toronto ; he has now gone to look into Lake
Huron by the way of Lake La Claye, and next winter we expect
a visit from him here, by way of the Bay of Kenty. You will,
before now, have been informed that the American Commissioners have failed in the purpose of their embassy to make
peace with the Indians, who would not agree to meet them at

all, unless they would previously consent to make the River Ohio the boundary between them and the United States. This is much to be regretted, from motives of humanity as well as the political consequences that may attend it, by making the Government of the States more urgent for the delivery of the posts, in order to overawe the Indians, and whenever this happens it will make a material change in the situation of the two Canadas, certainly not to their advantage.

To Isaac Todd, Esq.

KINGSTON, 1st October, 1794.

DEAR SIR,—It was with a mixture of surprise and indignation that I read an extract of a letter of yours this spring to the House in Montreal, and part of the one of 1st August to me, mentioning that Governor Simcoe had represented both Mr. Hamilton and myself as inimical to Government, and Mr. King's instance of the Marriage Act convinces me that it is not from the Minutes of the Council that the people at home could form such suspicions ; for there it will appear that this Act was brought into the House by myself, and that I was one of a Committee of Conference that induced the Lower House to withdraw their amendment.

It seems, then, that every man who will not be a mere tool, and pay implicit respect to the caprice and extravagance of a Colonial Governor, must be an object of jealousy and malevolence, not only here but at home. Yet ask these gentlemen for what purpose they gave me a seat in the Legislative Council ? I presume they will tell you it was from a desire to avail themselves of my knowledge of the country and acquaintance with the inhabitants, derived from long residence and familiar intercourse with them, to assist in framing such laws as might be most applicable to the situation of the colony ; not merely to show my complaisance to the person at the head of the Government.   Such, at all events, is the duty which I conceive that my appointment imposes on me ; and do they expect that I should either approve of or be silent upon measures that are totally inapplicable to the state of society in this country, that are inconsistent with its geographical situation, and must shock the habits and prejudices of the majority of its inhabitants ?

In the intercourse of private life I am disposed to be as accommodating as any man, but in the discharge of a public trust I must follow my own sense of duty and propriety.   I do not doubt the disposition of the Governor to consult the welfare of the Province, yet this disposition sometimes puts on an odd appearance.   He is a man of warm and sanguine temper, that will not let him see any obstacles to his views ; he thinks every existing regulation in England would be proper here.   Not attending sufficiently, perhaps, to the spirit of the constitution, he seems bent on copying all the subordinate establishments without considering the great disparity of the two countries in every respect.   And it really would not surprise me to see attempts made to establish among us Ecclesiastical Courts, tithes and religious tests, though nine-tenths at least of our people are of persuasions different from the Church of England, though the whole have been bred in a country where there was the most perfect freedom in religious matters, and though this would certainly occasion almost a general emigration.   One would, however, have thought that politics in the abstract would by this time have been sufficiently out of repute.   I did not expect or wish for the place I hold in the Legislature, nor do I care how soon I resign it ; but while I do retain it I will most certainly do my duty, re-

D

gardless of the smiles or frowns, the favours or the calumnies of any person whatever. Were I to act differently, I am sure you would be the first to despise me, and I certainly should despise myself—a degradation that would be poorly compensated by all the emolument or favour that could flow from a different line of conduct. All my prospects, as well for myself as my family, are confined to this Province ; I am bound to it by the strongest ties, and with its welfare my interest is most essentially connected. On this account, too, I cannot look tamely on and see measures pursued that by sowing the seed of discontent among us may ultimately avert from us the favour of Great Britain, which is so necessary to our prosperity. It is much to be regretted that Government seldom receives colonial information but through persons who too frequently are disposed to misrepresent both men and things.

Perhaps they were last spring reading imputations on my loyalty, while, in the discharge of my duty as a magistrate, I was addressing the following language to a Grand Jury :—

" We are happily exempt from those political dissensions that are now covering Europe with crimes and blood. Happy in a liberal constitution, and reposing under the protection of a Government from whose bounty we possess a soil that furnishes to the industrious every necessary of life—a Government that hath liberally assisted us in converting our forests into comfortable habitations and fruitful fields—we seem little disposed to forget, and base would we be if we could forget, the ties of gratitude as well as duty by which our allegiance is secured. We have therefore no public incendiaries to point out for your animadversion ; and I trust that the conduct of you, gentlemen, and others, in your private capacities, by discountenancing every insidious whisper or more open discourse that may tend to lessen in the people their attachment to the Government, will ever prevent the public peace from being disturbed in this way, with the necessity of judicial interference."

Such has been uniformly the tenor of all my public addresses, and also my private conversation when such topics have occurred. And though I do not think it necessary to bow with reverence to the wayward fancies of every subdelegate of the Executive Government, I will not hesitate to assert that His Majesty has not two more loyal subjects, and in this Province certainly none more useful, than Mr. Hamilton and myself, nor shall even the little pitiful jealousy that exists with respect to us make us otherwise. And though I hope we shall always have fortitude enough to do our duty, we are by no means disposed to form cabals, and certainly have not, nor do, intend wantonly to oppose or thwart the Governor. I am ashamed to have said so much on this subject, but I cannot help being provoked by such unhandsome conduct, and, besides, I am anxious to lay open to you my motives, for your approbation has always been of importance to me, and has become more so since my conduct is deemed of consequence enough to become the subject of misrepresentation among the people in power. It is, however, high time for me to proceed, in compliance with your wishes, to give you some further account of our legislative proceedings. In the transactions of our late session, the object most deserving of notice is our Judicature Bill, and two other Bills connected with it, for completing the scheme of administering civil justice among us. By the first all the former Courts are abolished, and every process for certain matters arising in any part of the Province above forty shillings must now be sued out and returned for trial at the Court which is to be held four times in the year at the seat of government. But a Court of concurrent jurisdiction has been established in every district, for the cognizance of matters of account and simple contract only, to the amount of £15, so that the plaintiff, if he pleases, may resort to the Supreme Court in every case, and must in all cases of trespass, or when damages are only consequential, or when special bail has been put in, be they ever so trifling. But pressed by the total want of professional men to set the machinery in motion, they have, at the very outset of the business, been reduced to the miserable expedient of qualifying by another Act, certain persons, to the number of sixteen, who are to be nominated by the Governor, to act as lawyers; and who, without any previous study or training, and by the mere magic virtue of the Privy Seal, are at once to start up adepts in the science of the law, and proficients in the intricate practice of Westminster Hall. This Bill was hurried through in a manner not very decent. My proposal to have it printed previous to discussion was overruled with some warmth and blustering; and you will be astonished to hear that a law of such importance, and, in conversation at least, disapproved by several of the members of the Lower House, should be passed through that House without debate, and in a single day. We are too much in a corner to pay any great respect to public opinion, or to trouble ourselves about saving appearances.

It is not yet in print, but I am sure, when it does appear, it will bear evident marks of its precipitate progress. The Court is to consist of the Chief Justice and two Puisne Judges, and to have all the powers incident to the King's Bench, Common Pleas, and Exchequer in England. The presidency of the Chief Justice in this Court renders our Court of Appeals a mere

name. Neither 'the Governor himself, nor our friends Mr.
Baby and Mr. Grant, nor the other members of the Executive
Council, are very deep lawyers. The Chief Justice will naturally be called on for his opinion, on which the decision must
be founded, and the business then is simply an appeal from
the Chief Justice in the King's Bench to the Chief Justice in
the Court of Appeals. The enclosed speech and protest will
show you the part I took in the business, and explain it to you
more fully. In the protest, Mr. Hamilton and myself had it
chiefly in view that the people at home should know the real
grounds of our opposition—a duty we owe ourselves, especially
since there exists a disposition to represent it as factions. The
same expense that this arrangement will occasion, by holding
the late District Courts only once in six months, and appointing one Judge of professional respectability to preside over two
districts, would have provided as effectually, and with infinitely more ease, for the due administration of justice, than the
present mode. And indeed, with the aid of all our new created
attorneys, I cannot yet see how business can be done with any
degree of convenience under this system in a country where the
intercourse between the different districts is casual at best, and
where, for five months in the year, the most populous parts of
the Province could more easily communicate with Europe than
with the seat of our government. Some further regulations
have been made respecting our militia, enabling the Governor
very properly to call them out by detachments, and to keep
them employed six months, either by land or upon the lakes ;
the other business related chiefly to matters of municipal
arrangement, except a tax on stills, very proper in itself,
and that may in time become productive. But the prodigality
of our Lower House will, I fear, greatly exceed our sources of

revenue. The trait I before mentioned of their passing the Judicature Bill in a single day must give you a better idea of these worthies than I could otherwise convey to you by writing a volume. And although we have yet no certain funds for the payment of the clerks and other officers of the two Houses, they have had the liberality to vote £600 to the Speaker for his past services, and a salary of £200 per annum in future. It is true the vote is conditional "if there are funds," but I fear it will be considered a sufficient pledge for creating them, and how this is to be done without greatly embarrassing our own little business, or involving us in difficulties with the Lower Provinces, exceeds my penetration to discover. Indeed, experience has almost made me a convert to Mr. Lymburner's opinion with respect to the division of the late Province of Quebec ; and his assertion that the country would be found unequal to support the expense of two Governments, at the rate our gentry proceed, will soon prove to have been too well founded. We are shortly to have a conference with the Lower Province on the subject of revenue, and in order to ascertain our share of the duty on wines imposed by the House of Assembly. Their commissioners have been nominated for some time, and are our friends James McGill, J. Richardson, Mr. J. Walker, Mr. Papineau, and another Frenchman whose name I do not recollect ; who ours are to be I know not, for our Governor has been lately so full of war and warlike arrangements as not to have thought much of the civil branches of his government, and no person having yet taken Mr. Osgoode's place the latter can at best go on but indifferently.

You are not unacquainted with Lord Dorchester's speech to the Indians, which I see has been the subject of parliamentary discussion, nor with the other causes of discontent existing between Great Britain and America, as well arising from transactions at sea as respecting the western posts and frontiers. Our Governor this spring erected a fort at the Miamis, of considerable strength, which has given great umbrage to our neighbours. General Wayne lately, after defeating the Indians, encamped around the fort a few days, but without attempting hostilities; he has withdrawn to the Glaize, where it is said he intends to fortify. In the meantime the militia of Detroit and Niagara were drafted, and reinforcements from the Rangers and 5th Regiment pushed on to Detroit, and we are in expectation that war would be kindled among us immediately. From this, however, we are relieved for the present; and as the season for action is almost over, I trust that all difficulties between the two Governments will be adjusted during the winter. In this hope I am strengthened by the accounts in the public prints of Mr. Jay's favourable reception; for however an American war might terminate in a national point of view, it must, at all events, be ruinous to this Province were it to have no other effect than that of merely calling away the inhabitants from the plough to the sword. In the action between the Americans and Indians, some of the Detroit militia, with Colonel Caldwell at their head, very imprudently joined the Indians; they had five men killed and several wounded. Among the former were McKillop, my quondam correspondent, and Charles Smith, Clerk of the Court at Detroit, both of whom, I believe, you knew. I send you two of our newspapers, in one of which you will find a list of the Acts passed during our late session, and the Governor's speech at the conclusion of it; the other, in the Loyal Association of the Home District, at the head of which is our friend Hamilton, contains a curious example to show how people can be led by a spirit of imitation, without regard to circumstances. This flourish, however, is, I believe, confined to head-quarters, and is certainly singular in its kind. I am afraid you will by this time be sick of so ver-bose a correspondent, but remember it is your own seeking, for I certainly should not otherwise have had the conscience to have obtruded upon you such a voluminous packet.

To Major Lothbridge.

KINGSTON, 10th Oct., 1794.

MY DEAR SIR,—I have been some time your debtor for your very friendly letter of 7th February last, which reached me in the latter end of June, at Niagara. I am much obliged by your political communications, and sorry that events would not warrant a more favourable account; and from those still more untoward ones that have reached us through the medium of the public prints, there seems reason to apprehend that the issue of the contest is not likely to prove favourable to the com-bined Powers. For, however glorious our naval victories, they seem rather to have ensured our own safety than to tend greatly to subdue the French. While occupied with the interesting scenes that are acting around you, in which the fate of Europe seems to be involved, our little local affairs can hardly claim your notice. To us, however, they lately ap-peared under a very unpleasant aspect; and some weeks ago we expected to have been ere now at war with our neighbours, the States. You have doubtless heard of Lord Dorchester's speech to the Indians, for I see it has been the subject of dis-cussion in Parliament, and will naturally suppose that it would not make a very favourable impression on the Americans, who were still further irritated by our building a fort about twelve miles up the Miamis River. On both these subjects very strong remonstrances were made to Mr. Hammond, and it was rather expected that under the immediate impulse of the ill-humour which they created, or at least fomented, some un-warrantable acts would have been committed on the frontiers. Indeed, they did go the lengths of stopping boats and seizing goods that were coming into the country by the way of Oswego, not, however, with the sanction of the Government. In the meantime General Wayne was advancing into the Indian country, and, either more prudent or more fortunate than his predecessors, baffled any attempts of the savages—and they made some pretty strong ones—to stop his progress. At length, about the latter end of August, he had got within a league of the fort; he was here attacked by the Indians, whom he had the address to draw into an ambuscade, and defeat, with considerable loss, however, on his side; while that of the Indians is said not to have exceeded twenty killed and about as many wounded. Among these, however, were some of the bravest of their Chiefs; and it seems to have discouraged and dispersed them as effectually as though the victory had been much more bloody.   In this engagement some of the Detroit militia very imprudently, and contrary to the orders of Major Campbell, who commanded the fort, mixed with the Indians and had five killed, one taken prisoner, and several wounded.   On the same day General Wayne encamped within a mile of the fort, and small parties of his people came oc-casionally very near and carried away some corn and hay from an island within gunshot.   During these transactions, the Governor, as you may suppose, was not idle.   Part of the Rangers and 5th Regiment were pushed on to Detroit; the Detroit and Niagara militia embodied, and we were in hourly

expectation of being engaged in actual hostilities. But the
removal of General Wayne to the Glaize, a principal settlement of the Indians, where it is said he is fortifying, has for
the present restored quiet, and we now learn with satisfaction
that Mr. Jay is to return with the olive branch ; for, however
the war might terminate as a national concern, to this Province
it must at all events have been ruinous.

Our Chief Justice, Mr. Osgoode, removed to Quebec in July
last, to take Mr. Smith's place, and his successor, if appointed,
has not yet made his appearance among us.

York, *alias* Toronto, it is said is to be the seat of government. The Governor and Mrs. Simcoe actually spent the last
winter there in their canvas house ; she has gone to pass the
ensuing one at Quebec ; he is at present at Detroit. Our
Province still continues its progress in improvement, and we
begin to think seriously of attempting to facilitate the export
of our produce to Montreal by means of scows and rafts ; for,
to say nothing of the expense by return batteaux, they are
really inadequate to the object. We cured here the last
season 480 barrels of pork for the use of the troops, and it is
thought double the quantity may be furnished this year. To
a brother member of a Land Board, we may be allowed, you
know, to talk of these things.

CHAPTER III.

SPEECH ON JUDICATURE BILL—DISTRICT COURTS SUITABLE FOR PRO-
VINCE—EXPENSE OF PROPOSED SYSTEM—BLACKSTONE ON COUNTY
COURTS—DISTANCE AN OBJECTION.

SPEECH ON THE JUDICATURE BILL, IN THE LEGISLATIVE COUN-
CIL, MONDAY, 16TH JUNE, 1794.

THERE is no maxim more incontestable in politics than that a
government should be formed for a country, and not a country
strained and distorted for the accommodation of a preconceived
or speculative scheme of government ; that in all the several
departments of it the arrangements should be calculated for
performing the business of the department in a manner the
least tedious and embarrassing to the public, rather than for
conferring splendour and emolument upon individuals. This is
a principle that every man who is called to the important business of legislation should bear constantly in mind, but more
especially so when he comes to deliberate respecting the mode
of administering justice, in which every individual is, more or
less, immediately interested. And as the British Legislature
has left us unrestrained in everything that does not militate
with the constitution they have given us, I apprehend we are
at perfect liberty, in the present instance, to pursue this principle to its full extent. Since the settlements which were
formed in this country after the American War began to
acquire any degree of stability, that part of the administration
of justice which relates to property and civil rights has been

managed by Courts of original and exclusive jurisdiction (subject to the revision of a Court of Appeals) erected in each of
the districts into which it has been divided. In these Courts
every cause might be, and has been, decided with very little
expense of time and money to the suitors ; how greatly to
their general satisfaction, let the solitary instance of a single
appeal determine. This arrangement was formed under the
auspices of a noble Lord who has ever bestowed the most
friendly and paternal attention to the welfare of this Province ;
and though I feel, from the experience of my own personal in-
capacity, that the Judges who preside in these domestic tribunals,
as I may without impropriety call them, may in one instance
at least be changed with advantage ; yet I do not hesitate to
affirm that, regard being had to the circumstances of the Province, the constitution of the Courts themselves can be altered
only for the worse. Yet this establishment, so well adapted
to the nature of the country, the present Bill is intended
totally to overturn, and to erect in its stead a system which,
by the expense, delays and embarrassments that must necessarily
attend it, will infallibly operate as a denial of justice in nine
out of ten, I had almost said ninety-nine out of a hundred
cases that our small and uncomplicated affairs are likely to
produce. In England, where the system now proposed to us
has long obtained, the " law's delay " has been frequently and
pathetically declaimed on as one of the great evils of life ; yet,
in point of size, England is hardly equal to the smallest of our
districts; the territory is compact and crowded with an immense
population ; the intercourse from the centre to the extremities,
and from one part to the other, is easy and expeditious; professional men swarm in every quarter ; and the City of London,
the great emporium of the commercial world, where the Court,

is fixed, furnishes of itself at least nineteen-twentieths of all the suits in the kingdom. But let us look around and see if there be in our situation the smallest analogy to this. With a thin population scattered over an immense extent of country, interrupted by inland seas and large tracts of unin-habited lands of from two to three hundred miles in extent, without communication or intercourse for at least five months in the year, with but a single lawyer within the compass of more than seven hundred miles, and where every part is equally barren of intricate or important subjects of litigation;—is there any similarity in the circumstances of the two countries? Can the same judicial arrangements be at all applicable to both?   To persist in the attempts to make them so will literally be bringing the mountain to Mahomet; or saying, like the famous tyrant of antiquity, " Here is our standard; if you are too long we will lop you, if you are too short we will stretch you to our dimensions."   But let us hear Mr. Justice Blackstone, with all the prejudices of a professional man about him, on the subversion of the County Courts in Eng-land; for even in England itself, for its infinitely smaller sub-division of counties, the system that now actually obtains in this Province was the original one, and was overturned, not by the calm, deliberate voice of legislation, but by the violence of in-vasion and conquest. After speaking of other changes that had been attended with the most injurious consequences, he says: " A third alteration in the English laws was by narrow-ing the remedial influence of the County Courts, the great seats of Saxon justice, and extending the original jurisdiction of the King's Justiciars to all kinds of causes arising in all parts of the kingdom. The constitution of this Court, and the Judges themselves who presided there, were brought from the Duchy of Normandy; and instead of the plain and easy method of determining suits in the County Courts, the chicanes and subtleties of Norman jurisprudence were introduced into the King's Courts, to which every cause of consequence was drawn." Here behold the change in contemplation completely anticipated. And if this Bill should pass, our posterity will find some future historian of the colony deploring, in similar language, the pernicious innovation, and reprobating the folly of our ill-judged acquiescence. For most unquestionably it will have the same effects upon our mode of administering justice that the Norman invasion had upon the English, except that from the great difference of local circumstances already stated, its operation must be proportionably much more injurious. For see it comes with all the *glorious* uncertainties of the law in its train, holding out wealth and distinction to the man of law, but poverty and distress to the unfortunate client. It comes with its multifarious actions of debt, covenant, account, assumpsit, case, trespass, trover and detinue—distinctions without essential difference, running into endless mazes where even the sages of the profession have themselves been frequently bewildered. It comes with all its hydra of demurrers, replications, rejoinders, surrejoinders, rebutters and surrebutters, and all the monstrous offspring of metaphysical subtlety begotten upon chicane, to swallow up our simple forms and modes of process which are easy to be understood and followed by any man of plain sense and common education. Here let us pause a moment and ask ourselves if this be indeed a desirable change. But admitting—what, however, is not intended— that these technical perplexities might be done away, let us examine simply the consequences that must inevitably result from the constitution of the Court itself. It is to be fixed, if we are to judge what has hitherto been, and what has been talked of as the seat of government, rather in the geographical centre of the colony than with any attention to its population. The eastern district at least, if not the western, far outnumbers in inhabitants the other districts, and, consequently, are likely to furnish the greatest number of lawsuits ; yet the man who has cause of action in the eastern or in the western district must travel from the River Raisin perhaps, or the River Trancke, across Lake Erie, or a hundred miles up the River St. Lawrence and across Lake Ontario, to sue out his process at Newark or York ; he must travel back with it, to put it into the hands of the Sheriff of the district whence he came ; the process must go back again to the place from whence it issued ; the defendant must resort thither to put in his pleas, and the plaintiff trudge back again to make his reply. Six months afterwards, it may be nine or twelve months, a Court of Assize may be held in the district where the cause originated, and the issue be tried by a jury if both parties are disposed to come to trial. But the matter ends not here ; the plaintiff or defendant, as either may have been so far successful, must the next term go back again and move for judgment, which he will probably obtain, unless he should be opposed by a motion for a new trial, or in arrest of judgment, which, if his money and patience holds out for another journey or two, may possibly be settled in a couple of terms more ; so that, on a moderate computation, if the parties do neither of them wish to protract the business, and are tolerably diligent, after spending a great deal both of their time and money, they may probably bring it to a conclusion in about two years. And with respect to the two most distant districts which I have named, it is hardly possible for the routine to be completed in a shorter time. But should any studied delay be interposed, it is impossible to foretell how long it may last. But gentlemen will perhaps say that this arrangement will soon bring lawyers among us, and then the business may be managed more expeditiously. Yes, we all know how anxious gentlemen of the law usually are to bring suits to a speedy termination. Yet, were this not the most palpable irony, as the same circle must be trodden round, I cannot see that, with their utmost diligence, the time I have calculated for the duration of a cause could be at all shortened. But admitting that it might in some degree, the business of the country is by no means equal to support respectable characters of the profession, and the House need not be told that the understrappers of it are the greatest pest that a society can be cursed with. I have thus endeavoured to point out some, for it is impossible to foresee and enumerate all the evils with which, under our circumstances, this Bill is pregnant. I trust, however, I have said enough to convince the House of its inexpediency, and to induce them to set their faces against it, as a measure, I will not say calculated, but certainly tending, to swell the importance and fill the pockets of the professors of the law, rather than promote the speedy and effectual administration of justice ; and that they will support me in the motion I now make, that this Bill be committed for this day three months.

CHAPTER IV.

LETTER TO DAVIDSON & CO.—SCARCITY OF LABOUR—HESSIAN FLY—
PRICE OF FLOUR AND PEAS—DISCONTENT IN LOWER CANADA—EX-
ECUTION OF M'LEAN—EXPORT OF POTASH AND STAVES—LETTER
TO GENERAL HUNTER—TRANSPORT TO MONTREAL—IMPROVEMENT
OF LACHINE—HEMP—LIST OF PRODUCE—LETTER FROM GENERAL
HUNTER—BRUYERE'S REPORT—LETTER TO MR. HAMILTON, LA-
CHINE—IMPROVEMENTS ACCOMPLISHED.

Messrs. Davison & Co.,
London.

KINGSTON, UPPER CANADA,
4th Nov., 1797.

GENTLEMEN,—I have been duly favoured with your Mr.
Palgrave's letter of the 10th March, and yours of the 27th
April and 11th July last, together with the public prints mentioned in the two first, for which and for your able and interesting sketch of public affairs be pleased to accept my sincere
thanks. I would gladly hope that before this time the convul-
sions which have so long agitated Europe have subsided, and
that the negotiations at Lisle have terminated in restoring that
peace so necessary to all the belligerent powers, and which
the withholding of specie at the bank, the late alarming meeting among the seamen, and the enormous expense of carrying
on the war, are very serious mementos that it will be prudence
on our part to purchase by any sacrifices consistent with the
national safety and honour. Independent of our general inte-
E

rest as a part of the British Empire, we look forward to a peace as to a period of particular prosperity for this Province, not only on account of the very considerable fall that it will occa- · sion in the price of every article of our importations, but from the expectation that on the reduction of the navy and army we shall receive a large accession of inhabitants better calculated for becoming orderly and well-affected settlers than the emigrants from the American Republic. In the present state of the country labour is not to be had at almost any price. The raising of two Provincial regiments has drained us of every man that would work for hire, and the cultivation of the farmer must consequently be circumscribed within the limits of that labour which his own family can supply. This cause has concurred with the ravages of the Hessian fly, and unfavourable seasons, to diminish very considerably our surplus produce. I believe the agent for purchases did not collect quite two thousand quintals of flour, though he got nearly a sufficiency of peas this spring ; the former he paid for at $4 per cwt., the latter at $1 per bushel, casks included, and no pork was advertised for. This, however, is not now a just criterion of what we have had to spare. The American garrisons and their settlements on Lake Ontario and Lake Erie have been almost wholly supplied with bread from this Province, at a rate considerably higher than the price paid by our Government. And our breweries and distilleries have consumed no inconsiderable portion of our grain ; the prices by this means have been so kept up that at this moment flour sells at 22s. 6d. per cwt. Indeed, although we have not suffered so much from the fly this season as we have done for a year or two before, a wet and backward spring and a very hot and dry summer have occasioned our wheat to be very much shrunk indeed, and to be consequently light and unproductive. Our peas and Indian corn, I understand, have turned out better, and I look forward to an increase of that valuable article, pork, in another year. I fear it is not at this time more abundant than it was last year, but the quantity is not now to be so easily ascertained as it was heretofore. The high prices given for this article in the new American settlements, and by the people engaged in the lumber business, have induced many of the principal farmers and the shopkeepers in the country to undertake the curing of it themselves. For this purpose it is not necessary to be so particular as when it is put up for the troops, and what there was to spare last year has generally been sold at $26 per bbl., and in some instances it has been sent to Lachine at that price for the purpose of victualling the batteau men in the merchants' service. Under these circumstances, you will see that the sending out provisions from England for the troops cannot be prejudicial to the Province just at this juncture, and in the situation that Lower Canada was in last winter, bordering upon revolt, it was certainly a matter of proper precaution in the Governor-General not to be in a state of dependence upon it for victualling the army. The execution of a Mr. McLean, one of Mons. Adet's emissaries, and other vigorous measures of General Prescott, have, however, effectually checked every seditious symptom among the Lower Canadians for the present. The demand for our produce at the American garrisons, and for their settlers, will of course be but temporary ; their own settlements near and along the lakes, it must be expected, will soon furnish enough for their troops, and become in a few years our competitors in the markets of this and the Lower Provinces. There being no place in the Province where lumber or potash are entered, it is impossilbe to

give you any accurate information of the quantity of these articles which we export. In estimating them at about one hundred and fifty tons of potash, and four hundred thousand
staves, exclusive of a large quantity of square oak timber, I
think I do not overrate them. The staves are principally of
that valuable kind called double butts, and are hewn smooth.
These are all sent to England, but there is a large quantity of
pine boards, plank and scantling, annually sent to Montreal,
and consumed there. The rafts into which these boards and
lumber are formed for the purpose of floating them down the
river have been occasionally used as vehicles for transporting
the potash to Montreal, and may be applied to any extent that
the circumstances of the Province may hereafter require for
the exportation of every article of its produce, from this and
other places further down the St. Lawrence, to the ports of
Lower Canada. About two-thirds of the potash, and nearly
the whole of the lumber, is supplied by the Eastern District,
which lies between this and Point au Bodet, the boundary of
the Lower Province. No potash has yet been manufactured,
nor has any person engaged in the lumber business, higher up
than the Bay of Kenty, an inlet extending from hence to the
westward about 60 miles, and from three-fourths of a mile to
two miles wide, with several deep bays branching from it in
different directions, bordering upon which are the principal
settlements that form what is called the Midland District. I
am much flattered by the obliging tender of your good offices,
which I shall not hesitate to avail myself of if anything should
occur that will require them. Not having a seaport in our
Province, it would be impossible or extremely inconvenient
for any person here to import goods except through the medium of a Montreal house. Goods must be there received, the

damages they have sustained at sea (as this sometimes happens) looked into and authenticated ; from thence they must be carted to Lachine, where boats and men are to be procured to transport them this far.   On the other hand, payments can be made there in bills or money when it would be difficult to convert them into remittances for England.   Furs must be there examined, sorted and baled ; potash inspected, and lumber culled.   The mode usually practised here is this : the merchant sends his order for English goods to his correspondent at Montreal, who imports them from London, guarantees the payment of them there, and receives and forwards them to this country for a commission of five per cent. on the amount of the English invoice.   The payments are all made by the Upper Canada merchant in Montreal, and there is no direct communication whatever between him and the shipper in London. The order, too, must be limited to dry goods, and he must purchase his liquors on the best terms he can in the home market ; and if he wishes to have his furs or potash shipped for the London market, he pays a commission of one per cent. on their estimated value ; if sold in Montreal, he is charged two and one-half per cent. on the amount of the sales.   This mode of business seems necessarily to be imposed upon us by our inland situation, but the terms upon which it has hitherto been conducted will become less burdensome when the mercantile capital of the country comes to bear a greater proportion to the trade of the country than it does at present.   In speaking of the situation and trade of the Province, these particulars of its mercantile intercourse with Europe naturally offer themselves to me, and to you they may not have been so obvious, and will not perhaps be unacceptable.

When we turn our view to New York, still greater difficulties occur ; among these are the very considerable duties laid upon almost every article entering the Atlantic ports, and which it is, from local circumstances, impossible to drawback upon exporting into this Province, without subjecting their revenue to frauds which no vigilance or custom-house restrictions could prevent.   And besides, I do not think, from the experience we have yet had, that the American treaty is likely to operate unfavourably upon the trade of even Lower Canada. Notwithstanding all the vapouring of our neighbours about the communication by the Mohawk River, it can never be made equal to that by the St. Lawrence even in its present state.   No mercantile house in the States has yet embarked in the trade of this country, and though there has been a number of petty adventurers, they have not frequently found their enterprises profitable, and in this part of the country they have latterly disappeared altogether.   On the contrary, some of the American merchants at Detroit are supplied with liquors and goods from Montreal, and I have seen casks of wine sent from thence directed for General Wilkinson, their Commander-in-Chief. Those merchants who were settled there while the place was under our jurisdiction have also considerably increased their importations through Montreal, and I mention with pleasure that they have almost unanimously elected to remain British subjects.   Whatever arbitrary or irregular acts may have occasionally been committed by some of our own military officers in that remote part of the country, they were soon effaced by the conduct of the Republican chiefs, who have at once declared the town of Detroit subject to military law, and have conducted themselves accordingly.

To His Excellency General Hunter.

KINGSTON, 24th Oct., 1801.

SIR,—I have the honour herewith to transmit to your Excellency an account of the different articles of provision, and the potash exported since the 20th April last, from this district, and from other parts of the Province to the westward, which may be relied on as accurate as far as it goes. The exports from that part of the Province which is situated between this and Lower Canada has been, in proportion, at least equally considerable, but I have no materials from which to form even a satisfactory conjecture of their amount. For there is no place there, as there is here, in which everything must centre previous to its exportation, and a great part is transported by the farmers themselves in sleds during the winter. Their average value in this account is stated rather below than above the truth, and when the price of the provisions furnished to Government for the use of the troops is added, it will compose a sum which, though a mere trifle in the immense aggregate of British commerce, will not appear contemptible when considered as arising from the rude produce of so recent an establishment. A large portion of these articles have been transported to Montreal on rafts of boards and timber and in scows, for the boats which transport the merchandise which we require no longer suffice for the export of articles of such comparatively great bulk and little value. Of these two modes of transport, that by scows will in future be preferred, as the flour on rafts cannot be kept dry, whereas in the scows it is equally secure as in common batteaux. These scows have carried to Montreal, and of course could carry to Quebec, from 350 to 400 barrels each, and might have taken 100 more as far as Lachine ; but ·
the water having been higher than usual during this summer,

has made the passage of the Lachine rapids more easy than is
to be expected in common seasons. These rapids have been
found the principal if not the only material obstruction in the
river to the safe and easy conveyance of our produce to the
ports of Lower Canada. The difficulties arising from the
scarcity of labour, which at present very much increase the
expense, time can only remove. But we hope, through the
assistance of your Excellency, that the navigation itself will
soon be facilitated. The improvement of the canals will do
much for the transport up, but the transport down is an object
at least equally important, and in this the canals are of no service. It will probably be found, upon examination by some
skilful engineer, that the channel in the Lachine rapids may,
without very great expense, be so improved as to render it perfectly safe for our scows and rafts in all seasons. But they lay
beyond the jurisdiction of our Legislature, and if they did not,
we have little in our power. From the Legislature of Lower
Canada I am not sanguine enough to expect much, and we can at
present look with confidence only to the liberality of Great
Britain for this among other means necessary to make this
Province as valuable to its inhabitants, and as useful to herself
in a commercial point of view, as its remote inland situation
will admit. Those who have been concerned in the scows, state
the expense, after deducting the price received for this vehicle
in Lower Canada, at about four shillings per barrel, but, as is
the case in all new undertakings, much expense has been
incurred that experience will now enable them to save ; and
they say that by getting the materials prepared in the winter,
and contracting with workmen in time, the expense of construction may be lessened nearly if not entirely one-half, and
that flour may in another season be floated down in this way

to Montreal at the comparatively moderate rate of half a dollar per barrel.   Nor is this the only benefit to be expected; for by getting them built in the neighbourhood of the mills, and other deposits of flour in the Bay of Kenty, they will save a great part of the expense now incurred for transport in the small vessels which have hitherto been used to carry it to this place.   By means of large grooved cases reaching from side to side, they may be fitted for transporting wheat and other grain in bulk, and may be adapted by-and-bye for the secure transportation of our hemp, which I expect will be added to our exports at no very distant period.   There is every disposition to give it a fair trial in this district, and Alexander Fisher, Esq., of Adolphustown, is preparing to sow from twelve to fifteen acres in the manner that is pointed out by the Society for the Encouragement of Arts, &c., and in the hope of obtaining the premium offered by that patriotic Society; but seed is wanting.   I some time since wrote to Mr. McGill, whom your Excellency has appointed, jointly with Mr. Smith, to apply and distribute the Provincial grant for this purpose.   His answer, which I send herewith, is not very encouraging; and as I learn from another quarter that their agent, Mr. Swezy, had not, unless very lately indeed, proceeded on his mission, I fear much that this part of the Province is not likely to benefit in time by any supplies which he may procure; and I take the liberty to suggest the expediency of sending us some in the meantime from Lower Canada, to prevent our ardour from cooling.

I intended to have sent your Excellency this account sooner, but some of the gentlemen from whom I was to collect my information were absent.

I have the honour to be, with the greatest respect and esteem,

Sir,

Your Excellency's very obedient servant,

RICHARD CARTWRIGHT.

ACCOUNT OF FLOUR AND OTHER ARTICLES OF PRODUCE SHIPPED FOR MONTREAL BY THE RESPECTIVE MERCHANTS OF KINGSTON IN 1801.

BY WHOM FORWARDED.	Produce of Kingston and parts adjacent.				From Niagara.		From Detroit.	
	Fine and Superfine Flour.	Middlings.	Potash.	Peas.	Fine and Superfine Flour.	Potash.	Fine and Superfine Flour.	Potash.
	Bbls.	Bbls.	Bbls.	Bus.	Bbls	Bbls.	Bbls.	Bbls.
R. Cartwright...............	2453	282	96	77	1150	......	613	
J. Cumming	729	10	14	......	1375	14	773	
Peter Smith......	965	......	100	150	524			
T. Markland..................	719	......	18	75				
L. Herkimar	250							
John Kirby & Co.	342	......	43					
J. Forsyth, for self and Robins	803	......	......	......	298	......	1103	6
Do for B. Seymour ...	250							
J. Robins, for self, Son and E. Smith..................	431	......	9					
D. McDonell	523	30	34	50	43	37		
Do for W. Washburn	249	......	8					
Do for B. Seymour..	100	......	40					
Do for J. McNab	140	......	65					
Do for J. Barton	150							
Total	8084	322	427	352	3390	51	2489	6

NOTE.—There is besides 350 bushels wheat from Mr. Crooks, and 500 lbs. cheese from Mr. Hamilton, of Niagara, 72 lbs. hogs' lard from R. Cartwright, and 1000 lbs. butter from Mr. Smith and others from Kingston, besides staves, boards and lumber.

RECAPITULATION.

13,963 bbls. Fine and Superfine Flour, @ 35s................	£24,435	5	0
322 " Middlings, or 2nd Flour,	" 23s. 4d............	375	13	4
350 bus Wheat,	" 6s. 8d............	116	13	4
352 " Peas,	" 5s.	88	0	0
484 bbls. Potash,	" 90s	2,178	0	0
1,000 lbs. Butter, 500 lbs. Cheese,	" 1s.	75	0	0
78 " Hogs' lard,	" 8d.	2	12	0
17,000 Oak Staves,	" £28	476	0	0
Pine and Cedar timber, quantity not ascertained, sold for about		120	0	0
Province Currency............£27,867	3	8

From His Excellency General Hunter.

QUEBEC, 24th Nov., 1801.

DEAR SIR,—It gives me pleasure to find, from the return enclosed in your letter to me of 20th Oct., that the articles of provisions, potash, &c., exported from Kingston during the last summer, amount to so considerable a sum as you have therein stated. Under circumstances of equal industry and success, there is no doubt but the farmers and others concerned in the export trade will be rendered easy and affluent in the course of a few years. I lost no time, upon the receipt of your letter, in ordering a careful examination of the Lachine rapids by Captain Bruyere, Royal Engineer, assisted by two of the best pilots, on the communication between Lachine and Montreal. A copy of Captain Bruyere's report to Colonel Mann upon that subject I enclose herewith for your information. Although it appears from Captain Bruyere's report that the removing the rocks and shoals, for the purpose of rendering the navigation for loaded boats and rafts more easy and safe, is nearly if not quite impracticable, yet the report affords some useful hints to all concerned in the construction of rafts, scows, &c. As Colonel Mann will, early in the ensuing spring, visit the works now carrying on at the Cascades, I shall direct him to inspect the Lachine rapids himself, and if his report should be favourable to the removal or lessening the present obstructions, I shall have much pleasure in doing everything in my power towards facilitating so desirable an object. I have no doubt but the cultivation of hemp in Upper Canada will succeed beyond our most sanguine expectations, when the difficulty of procuring good seed in sufficient quantities can be got over. I have the firmest reliance on the exertions of the Commissioners appointed by me for that purpose. When sleighing begins, they will, no doubt, distribute among the farmers in the several districts of the Province what seed they have purchased, which will be in sufficient time for sowing it in the spring. In Lower Canada no hemp seed can be procured for any price; Mr. Clarke, at Montreal, raised about 40 bushels of hemp seed, but the whole of that quantity must remain for the disposal of Sir Robert Milnes, who advanced money for the experiment.

I am, &c.,

P. HUNTER.

To R. Hamilton.

KINGSTON, 14th May, 1806.

DEAR SIR,—You will be pleased to learn that, notwithstanding the impracticability stated by Lt. Bruyere, in his report to Col. Mann, the *three large rocks* which formed so considerable an impediment in the rapids of Lachine have been blown to pieces and removed; and that by making a dyke or embankment upon the principles stated by you and Mr. Clarke in summer of 1804, the water was at once raised from ten inches to three feet. All this has been done for £600, and the work has stood the test of one winter. It is proposed to extend it considerably this summer, and Mr. Auldjo, who is one of the Commissioners, tells me that he has no doubt that by this means there will always be at least three feet of water in the channel. They have remaining £400 of last year's appropriation, to which the Legislature have this season added £1,000, so that there is £1,400 for this object alone; and they have besides given the sum of £500, if I recollect aright, for other parts of the river between that and Coteau du Lac. Say, therefore, what they will of the House of Assembly of Lower Canada, these are no bad specimens of their public spirit.

R. C.

CHAPTER V.

LETTER TO GEN. SIMCOE—GRANTS OF LAND—ACTION OF LAND BOARD—
DELAY IN ISSUING PATENTS—PROPOSED MEASURES OF RELIEF—
LETTER TO MR. M'GILL— PATENTS TO ISSUE—DEEDS DESTROYED—
RECENT ACTS—QUARREL OF HOUSES.

REPESENTATION RESPECTING THE STATE OF LANDED PROPERTY,
IN UPPER CANADA, DELIVERED TO GENERAL SIMCOE, JULY,
1795.

THE settlements in the now Province of Upper Canada were
begun in the year 1784, after the 24th of June in that year,
when the lands, by the bounty of His Majesty, were distributed
in certain regulated proportions to the disbanded troops and
loyalists who had joined the royal standard.   Each person, or
more frequently two persons in conjunction, received a certificate signed by the Governor, and countersigned by the Surveyor General or Deputy Surveyor General, declaring that
A. B. being, by His Majesty's instructions, entitled to a certain
quantity of land, had drawn Lot No. 1, or part of said lot, as
the case might be, in a certain concession of a certain township
or seigniory, and being settled and having improved thereon,
he should at the end of twelve months receive a deed of concession authorizing him to alienate the same.   The grantee
having complied with the condition, by settling and improving
his location, became evidently entitled to his deed, and had,
in equity and justice, at least a right to dispose of the lands
so ceded to him.   From the very mistaken plan of generally

giving but 100 acres together to any persons, the people soon
found themselves straitened in their locations, which were too
small to make good farms ; various exchanges were made in
consequence, upon principles of mutual accommodation, in order
to increase the size of the farms to two hundred acres and
upwards.

Besides the very numerous transfers that were made for this
principle, persons who had obtained land for their families, or
on other accounts, had a larger portion than they immediately
wanted, were disposed to sell a part in order the better to enable them to improve the remainder, and a variety of other
causes which constantly operate in shifting property from hand
to hand induced the loyalists to part with a portion of theirs,
or frequently to mortgage it, to enable them to obtain the con-
veniences or even the necessaries of life. Thus matters were
conducted till the year 1789, when, upon suggestions from the
Land Boards, which had been appointed in the preceding year
in the several districts, " that people came in from the States
to apply for lands without any intention to settle them, but
merely to make money by the sale of them," certificates were
sent up to be issued by them, declaring lands so granted to be
forfeited if not settled upon within the year, and particularly
expressing that they and all others of a similar nature were not
transferable unless by the sanction of the Land Board. This
was principally intended to prevent the abuse above-mentioned,
and was further useful, as far as it went, to authenticate sales or
assignments among the settled inhabitants. But this had no
retrospective operation, and could not attach upon the large
additional grants of lands to officers, to whom the Boards could
regularly issue no certificates, nor to those townships where,
through the neglect of the Surveying Department, the settlers

had nothing but a ticket barely expressing the number of the lot. Ten years had thus elapsed before any preparations for granting the patents were in forwardness, and such have been the mutations of landed property, if indeed it can be so called, that very few inhabitants of the Province are unconcerned in them. That patents were not issued agreeable to the tenor of the certificates was not the fault of the people, and if they should now be delivered to the original holders of the certificates, the whole country will be thrown into confusion. The strongest temptations will be held out to fraud and avarice, and all the mutual confidence between the people destroyed, and such heats and animosities be kindled as may be attended with the most pernicious consequences ; for although, on complying with the terms of the certificate, the holder had in justice the entire and complete property of the soil, to do therewith as he pleased, yet, in the technical precision of the law, the delivery of the patent completely overturns every prior sale or exchange—even those sanctioned by the Land Boards perhaps not excepted—invalidates every mortgage, and gives a power to the party, his heirs or subsequent assigns, to eject the person who may have made a *bona fide* purchase, and who may have expended in improvements twenty-five times the original value of the soil. These are evils that every friend to the Province must deprecate, and should interpose to prevent if possible, and the attempt would come forward with peculiar propriety under the auspices of the Executive Government, as a most agreeable and popular measure. Indeed, from the 44th and 45th clauses of the Act of Parliament establishing the Constitution of this Province, it would seem that the Legislature of Great Britain considered the certificates as actual grants, and so did the Legislature of Lower Canada,

for in an Act passed in the 33rd year of His Majesty's
reign, intituled "An Act to continue the ordinances regulating the practice of the law, and to provide more
effectually for the dispensation of justice, and especially
in the new districts," part of the 12th clause establishes
regulations for the mode of advertising the sale of real
estates seized in execution. But as the certificates have
not, either in the one case or the other, been declared to
convey an assignable title, they still rest upon their own
foundation, only that these Acts seem strongly to countenance
the propriety of confirming all fair and honest alienations made
under these certificates.   For this purpose it is proposed to be
enacted, "That all *bona fide* sales or mortgages of lands to
which the settler or mortgagor had a just claim by having complied with the conditions on which the lands were ceded to him
by His Majesty's instructions, shall be good and valid in law,
although no patent had actually been granted for the same,
and that no patent which shall hereafter be granted for such
lands shall be deemed to invalidate any title or claim under
such sale or mortgages as aforesaid.   That it shall be sufficient
evidence of such *bona fide* sales if the same shall have been
made under the sanction of the Land Board, regularly endorsed
on the certificate, or by deed of sale under the hand and seal
of the Sheriff when sold by process of law, or by a written instrument under the hand and seal of the party, subscribed by
two witnesses, or by assignment on the certificate itself under
the hand of the party, and attested by two subscribing witnesses.
And that it shall be sufficient evidence of such *bona fide* mortgages, that they have been given under the hand and seal of
the party, in the presence of two subscribing witnesses : Provided that such sales and mortgages shall be entered in the

Register Office of the district in which the lands are situated, within one year after the passing of this Act, or within one year from the establishment and opening of such office, otherwise the holders shall be deprived of the benefit of this Act. That all lands held under certificates of occupation shall be liable to claims under judgment of a Court of law, rights of inheritance, or otherwise, in the same manner as they would have been if held by patent under the Great Seal. That these provisions shall have only a retrospective operation from the passing of this Act, or refer only to such transactions as may have taken place before the 1st of January last. That the lands so transferred or assigned shall be liable to the payment of all fees due for grants of the said lands to the officers of the Crown, provided they were originally held by such persons as were liable to the payment of such fees, and the possessor shall have recourse upon the vendor for repayment of such fees, provided there has been no stipulation between them to the contrary."

The claims to lands as above stated have been provided for in a different and perhaps a better mode by laws passed from time to time to authorize commissioners to hear and report on such claims, and allowing the patents to issue in favour of the person whose claim was 'duly established before such commissioners.

James McGill, Esq.

KINGSTON, 12th July, 1800.

DEAR SIR,—My letters to the House will have informed you of my arrival once more under my own shed on the 10th instant, where I had the satisfaction of finding all well. I have been at Niagara and saw H. W. Dickson, who says the patents shall be sent me as soon as they can be made out. The whole winter's

F

labour at the different offices has been thrown away, and about
eight hundred deeds prepared for the Governor's signature have
become waste paper, from his refusal to put his name to them.
He has determined that they shall be upon parchment, that
they shall contain the complete and legal designation of the
grantee, be expressed as to the number of acres, &c., in letters
instead of figures, and free from those erasures and interline-
ations with which they have too generally been disgraced.
That General Hunter should make a point of this will not surprise you ; the wonder rather is, that such culpable negligence
should be tolerated so long.   I have already informed you that
we had passed a temporary law to authorize the Executive Government to take such steps as might be deemed expedient to
collect such duties as we were by treaty authorized to levy on
articles imported from the United States, and which I presume
will be speedily acted upon.   We have also passed a law for
arranging the representation of the Province more conform-
able to existing circumstances, and by which the members of
the Assembly are augmented to twenty, and in which it is provided that none but *bona fide* British subjects shall vote at the
ensuing election who have not been four years personally resident in the Province and taken the oath of allegiance, nor at
any subsequent election unless they have been seven years previously resident.   Some others of less importance have also been
agreed on, but General Hunter has thought it necessary to reserve two of the most consequence for His Majesty's pleasure :
one of which defines the different objects to be rated in our
County assessments, and fixes their value ; and the other calculated to prevent an effect which certainly was not intended, and
which yet must necessarily follow from several persons having
been frequently joined as grantees of certain parcels of land in

one deed, by which they become joint tenants, and which gives a right to the survivor to take the whole, instead of each having in severalty their distinct and separate portions, which was evidently the intention of the Crown. The Council and the Assembly have parted on very ill terms with each other, and I was unfortunate enough to differ with the majority of my brethren, and to think our conduct towards the House of Assembly neither decent or warrantable. I see that in your Province, though the fund is raised by the Legislature in general, the appropriations are annually made by vote of the House of Assembly, and paid in consequence of an address from them to the Governor to issue his warrant, &c. Now, this point was given up by our Commons, and a Bill brought in for the appropriations, specifying the salaries of the officers of the two Houses, &c. To this, amendments were carried in our House to strike out £150 for printing the Journals of the Assembly ; £4 10s. incurred for printing an Act brought forward in the course of the preceding session, that the public might become acquainted with its purport and tendency ; and £5 odd to the Sergeant-at-Arms for contingencies, under pretence that the particular items of the account had not been submitted to our inspection. It has not, I believe, been very usual for a House of Commons to be so treated ; and without entering into the question about our right to control the expenditures of the Assembly in matters particularly relating to their own proceedings, I could not help thinking that in the case before us the attempt to exercise it was neither necessary nor proper. On receiving back the Bill with our amendments, the Commons were all in a flame, and voted that their proceedings relative to it should be expunged from their journals, and we were the next day prorogued ; so that unless healing measures be adopted in our next Parliament, we have a comfortable prospect before us. At the hazard, however, of the imputation of sacrificing to popularity, I must say that I think our House were the aggressors ; and the best way of supporting our own consequence and privileges is certainly not to encroach on the privileges of the Assembly. I did not think, when I began, that my letter would have been of its present length, but you will probably have no objections to have some idea of what we have been doing, and I have been as brief as possible.

I remain, my dear Sir,
Yours very sincerely,
RICHARD CARTWRIGHT.

CHAPTER VI.

LETTER TO GENERAL HUNTER — FIRST SETTLERS LOYALISTS AND
TROOPS—RELATIVES OF LOYALISTS ADMITTED, 1788—EMIGRANTS
INVITED BY GOVERNOR SIMCOE—OBJECTIONS—PROPOSED REMEDY
—IMPROPER EMIGRATION.

To His Excellency General Hunter.

KINGSTON, 23rd August, 1799.

SIR,—From the conversations with which I have been honoured
by your Excellency, I am induced to present you with the following sketch of the history and present state of the population
of this Province, together with some suggestions respecting the
means of its amelioration.   Your Excellency is already aware
that the settlement of this Province was originally suggested
by the propriety and necessity of providing an asylum for the
American Loyalists after the peace of 1783.   Those who were
already in the Province of Quebec were afterwards joined by a
considerable number from New York, who preferred this country to Nova Scotia, and there were further added to them
several of the German troops, and some of the disbanded
soldiers of the British regiments.   The great mass of this
population was settled between the Point of Bodet and the
head of the Bay of Kenty ; for except the single regiment of
Butler's Rangers, and the persons attached to the Indian Department, there were none to settle the country in the neighbourhood of Niagara and Detroit, and the North sides of Lake
Erie and Lake Ontario were left wholly uninhabited.   For the

four first years the strictest attention was paid, not to admit
any other description of persons as settlers; but in the year
1788 some little relaxation took place in this particular, and it
having been represented to Lord Dorchester that there were
in the States many relations of the Loyalists as well as other
persons, who, although they had not joined the Royal standard,
were, however, well affected to the British Government, his
Lordship was pleased to give it as an instruction to the Boards
which he at this time established in each of the four districts into which the new settlements had been recently divided, for the purpose of inspecting the details of the land
granting business therein, to examine into the loyalty and good
character of such persons as were disposed to become settlers,
and if they appeared to be unexceptionable in these respects,
to give them a certificate of location for a lot of not more than
two hundred acres, under the express condition of becoming
bona fide settlers.   Thus many useful inhabitants were gradu-
ally acquired; and if now and then any improper character
slipped in by surprise, the danger was small, as he would be
kept in order by a well-disposed neighbourhood.   In this train
affairs continued till this country was made a separate Province,
and General Simcoe sent over to govern it.   He appears to
have thought that the immediate peopling of the country was
an object of sufficient importance to supersede the regulations
which had been hitherto observed in distributing the waste
lands of the Crown.   A proclamation was immediately issued
for the purpose of inviting emigrants, and the speculations in
lands being about this time at their height in the American
States, jobbers flocked in from every quarter, proposing to
bring a large number of settlers, and the Loyalists heard, with
astonishment and indignation, persons spoken of as proprietors

of townships whom they had encountered in the field under
the banners of the rebellion, or who had been otherwise no-
toriously active in promoting the American revolution. For-
tunately, however, their diligence or ability to fulfil their promises was not equal to their assurance in making their appli-
cations ; and so little was done in the course of several years
towards the actual settlement of a large number of townships
which had been reserved for these speculators and their associ-
ates, that the Government in 1797 considered themselves at
liberty to dispose of them otherwise.   In the meantime a considerable number of people were brought into the country of a
very different description from the original settlers, and the
functions of the Land Boards having been put an end to in the
year 1794, every application for lands was afterwards made
immediately to the Executive Council, who of course exercised a discretion with respect to the character of the appli-
cant, and the quantum of the grant that the Boards were not
competent to, and it has so happened that a great portion of
the population of that part of the Province which extends from
the head of the Bay of Kenty upwards is composed of persons
who have evidently no claim to the appellation of Loyalists.
I will not disguise from your Excellency the opinion which I
have always entertained, and on every proper occasion expressed,
that this ought never to have been permitted.   One necessary
consequence has been to dispel the opinion fondly cherished by
the Loyalists, that the donation of lands to them in this country was intended as a mark of peculiar favour and a reward
for their attachment to their Sovereign ; for how could such an
idea remain upon their minds, when they afterwards saw them
lavished upon persons who had such pretensions ?

  This, however, is not the greatest evil. In all establishments of a political nature, it is of more consequence to lay a solid foundation than to give them a sudden and premature celebrity. In the founding of a colony, the character of the inhabitants seems to be much more material than their numbers; these, in the course of time, will be sufficiently multiplied by natural causes, that, if originally faulty, is not so easily changed. It must be admitted that the Americans understood the mode of agriculture proper for a new country better than any other people, and being, from necessity, in the habit of providing with their own hands many things which in other countries the artizan is always at hand to supply, they possess resources in themselves which other people are usually strangers to ; and boldly began their operations in a wilderness, when the dreary novelty of the situation would appal an European. But their political notions in general are as exceptionable as their intelligence and hardihood are deserving of praise. I am not, however, inclined to impute to such of them as emigrate to this Province either hostile or treacherous views; but it would be an error equally as great to suppose that they are induced by any preference they entertain for our government. They come probably with no other intent than to better their circumstances, by acquiring lands upon easy terms. Now, it is not to be expected that a man will change his political principles or prejudices by crossing a river, or that an oath of allegiance is at once to check the bias of the mind, and prevent the predilection for those maxims and modes of estimating and conducting the concerns of the public to which he has been trained, from displaying itself, even without any sinister purpose, whenever an opportunity shall be presented. It would be cruel and invidious to point this to individual instances. But the principle is founded on human nature, and its operation ought to be calculated upon in every political combination. Indeed, the Government, even while throwing wide the door to invite them, seem to have been in some measure aware of this, for an Act was brought forward by the Attorney-General in the House of Assembly, and passed in the year 1795, to prevent such persons from being eligible to a seat in that House till after a residence of seven years within the Province—a feeble and temporary palliative to a radical disease which it would have been easier to prevent than it will be to cure. Let us see, however, if any more effectual remedy can be applied. The best that occurs to me will be to settle among the emigrants of this description men of tried loyalty, and who have been bred up in habits of subordination, in sufficient numbers to discountenance that affectation of equality so discernible in the manner of those who come to us from the American republic. It would seem that the French will not be able much longer to disturb the repose of the world, and it is probable that a peace which will crown Great Britain with everlasting laurels will also leave her with a number of deserving men to provide for. And here I cannot but regret that the whole of the first range of townships along Lake Ontario and Lake Erie are preoccupied. Those, however, extend only twelve miles towards the interior part of the country, and there is beyond them land equally fertile, though not so conveniently situated. To those who can and will cultivate them, they will soon furnish a comfortable subsistence. In the meantime the high price of labour, which is not less than eight or ten dollars per month for common servants, and from a dollar to a dollar and a quarter for carpenters, masons, etc., per day, will soon enable a man who comes without anything but his health, and frugal and industrious habits, to acquire a few cattle and other articles necessary for improving and stocking a farm. If Government, therefore, gives him the land, and provides a passage, together with a few months' provisions to guard against contingencies, it will not be necessary to go to any further expense. Indeed, there is at this moment in the public stores of the Province a large quantity of various kinds of implements of husbandry and materials for building that cannot be so well disposed of in any other manner as by being distributed to this description of persons. Should they have families, they will thrive the faster, for here, instead of being a burden, a numerous family of children ensures the prosperity of their parents—the boys, by their labour in the field ; the girls, by their assistance in the dairy and the coarser kinds of household manufactures. If there should be a few persons of a liberal education, and manners calculated to make them respectable, part of the reserves of the Crown in some of the townships already occupied could not, perhaps, be better disposed of than by being allotted to them. These reserves are so situated that the occupants would be interspersed in the most desirable manner among the other settlers, and would enable the Government to make a proper selection of Justices of the Peace and other officers necessary for the support of good order in the different parts of the colony. In the distribution of lands not less than two hundred acres should be given to every man—a smaller quantity will not be sufficient to make him a good farm—and fifty acres more for each member of his family, if he has one, will not be an improper augmentation. Supposing that a scheme of this kind should be approved of by His Majesty's Ministers, I think the number of persons sent at one time should not be very great, and that measures should be previously concerted with the Colonial Government for their reception and accommodation. A very large number might not at once be properly accommodated or fall into immediate employment, and in that case the time unavoidably taken up in marking out to each their locations would be tedious and discouraging; and it would be desirable to avoid everything likely to increase that discomfort which, however favourable his future prospects may be, the needy emigrant must inevitably encounter for a while in every strange country. The greatest precaution also should be used to exclude improper persons from the projected emigration. I take the liberty of mentioning this from a notorious instance of the neglect of it which occurred in the year 1792. In that year a considerable number of persons were sent from England, under the denomination of Loyalists, provided in the most ample manner with bedding and clothing, with nails, hinges, &c., for building, and with the necessary implements of husbandry, and with orders to be victualled for three years from the King's stores. With a few exceptions, one would have supposed that London had been ransacked to collect the idle and the profligate. The donations of the Government were very generally disposed of to procure the means of gratifying their passion for ardent spirits, and when they could no longer resort to the King's stores for provisions, some of them enlisted, others abandoned the Province, or in some instances became a burden upon the inhabitants for support. I am perfectly warranted in asserting that there are not more than a dozen families of them now settled in the Province, and some of these are in no very good repute. Thus has the liberality of the Government been perverted, and a very considerable expense been thrown away, which, applied to proper objects, would have placed them in easy circumstances, and added greatly to the flourishing state of the colony.

I have thus candidly given your Excellency my sentiments on this subject; but while I have expressed them without reserve, it has been far from my intention to cast the slightest degree of obloquy upon any of those who may not have viewed it precisely in the same light with myself.

I am, &c.,

RICHARD CARTWRIGHT.

CHAPTER VII.

REPORT OF COMMISSIONERS—DUTIES ON WINES—PROPORTION SET-
TLED ON BASIS OF POPULATION—LETTER TO MR. LEES—DUTIES
ON AMERICAN GOODS IMPOSSIBLE—LETTER TO MR. M'GILL—DE-
PRECATES PROTECTION.

REPORT OF THE PROCEEDINGS OF THE COMMISSIONERS FOR
SETTLING DUTIES, &C., IN 1795.

AFTER some preliminary correspondence relative to the place
of meeting, the undersigned Commissioners met the Commissioners of the Province of Lower Canada at Montreal on the
13th day of February, and continued their conferences till the
18th day of the same month, when they were terminated by
the provisional agreement now before the House, to which we
also beg leave to submit the principal motives and arguments
by which we were induced to subscribe to this agreement.

The first object of our appointment being to ascertain our
proportion of certain duties collected upon wines in the Lower
Province during the years 1793 and 1794, the Commissioners
of that Province produced an account, a copy of which is here-
to annexed, containing an accurate statement, as far as could
be collected, of all the wines sent into this Province, distin-
guishing those sent by the Ottawa River from those sent by
the River St. Lawrence. We claimed the duty on the whole
quantity, insisting that the passing into our geographical limits
was the proper criterion for determining our proportion ; and
as we could establish custom-houses to enforce our demands,

there could be no pretence for disputing them. To this it was answered, that however true these positions might be in general, and when applied to sovereign and independent States, yet they would not always hold good between dependencies of the same Empire, especially under the peculiar circumstances and relations of these two Provinces ; that if power and right were to be considered as synonymous, they were not accountable to us for any part of the present duty, or any other that they might be disposed to lay hereafter, but upon this principle each Province must be left to pursue their own plans, regardless of the other ; that though they had nothing to fear from a contest of this kind, they, however, were disposed to do everything that could reasonably be expected to shun it, and were willing to give us as large a share of the revenue arising from the duties upon their imports as we could in justice claim ; that, therefore, they had no objections to our receiving the duty upon every article of this kind transported by the River St. Lawrence, whether for the consumption of the inhabitants or for the Indian trade, but that they could not make us any such allowance upon articles transported by the Ottawa River, which barely passed along the extreme limits of our Province, and through a very small and uninhabited portion of it, to be traded with remote and independent tribes of Indians ; for that this would, in fact, be taxing their capital and industry for our benefit, and deriving a revenue from a source which, but for their exertions, would have no existence. We replied that our negotiation was to be conducted upon principles of equity ; and, though we were not disposed to give up the just claims of our Province, we had no wish to involve the two Provinces in a contest that would be injurious and disreputable to both, by insisting upon demands that were not reasonable ; but that if the distinction of geographical limits was once laid aside, it would not be easy to make any proper discrimination ; that it might, perhaps, as well be said that the trade by the St. Lawrence was carried on by the capital of Lower Canada as the trade by the Ottawa River, and that we could not see that there were just grounds for making the difference they contended for.

To this they answered that the difference was palpable and striking ; that the trade by the former route not only found convenience and protection from the extensive tract of settled country which it passed through, but was for the most part carried on by the industry and for the benefit of persons resident in the Upper Province ; and whenever the trade by the Ottawa River should derive the same benefit from establishments of ours, and be carried on by the agency of persons resident amongst us, they should be very willing to admit our claims to their full extent, but that at present they derived not the smallest protection or advantage from any establishment of ours ; that every person engaged in this business was brought from Lower Canada ; and with respect to the particular article in question, that it was not even made an article of trade, but was carried as the private stores of the persons employed in this trade. To put this question in a proper light, they would ask, Was it reasonable, was it just, that the Province of Lower Canada should pay a sum of money to the Province of Upper Canada for liberty to trade with the Indians in the country about the Hudson's Bay or on the Mississippi ? The arguments prevailed with us to give up our claim for the present upon articles transported by the Grand River ; and as they forebore to urge any allowance for leakage or abatement on account of wines sent into this Province on

which no duty had been paid, we agreed to accept of the sum
of £333 4s. 2d. as our proportion of the duty upon wines.
The next object was to fix upon a principle for arranging our
future proportion of this or such other duties as might be hereafter imposed. For this end various expedients were mentioned,
such as a declaration upon oath to be made by persons forward-
ing goods to Upper Canada, or that every bill of lading should
express the quantity of dutiable articles, and duplicates of these
be deposited with some person to be appointed for that purpose
at Lachine; but these were found to be liable to too much
uncertainty, and could not possibly attach upon that part of
the trade carried on by the farmers, or other persons not established merchants, who resort themselves to Montreal for
their supplies.   An officer at the Point of Bodet was next
proposed; but besides the expense of such an establishment,
which was a very material objection, it was considered as likely
to occasion much delay and embarrassment to the trade of the
two Provinces, and to become a source of discord between them,
for to make it effectual there must be a power to stop, to
search and confiscate, and besides, by a change in the road in
the eastern district which is in contemplation, it would be
rendered wholly useless in the winter.   A certain determinate
proportion was then recurred to, and it was unanimously agreed
that, all circumstances considered, the respective population of
the two Provinces would form the most eligible, if not the
most equitable principle of agreement, and that this might be
considered in the proportion of one to seven.   This at once super-
sedes the necessity of officers and salaries that must otherwise
have absorbed, unavoidably, a large portion of the revenue, and
probably have created dissensions between the Provinces.   It re-
moves at once every clog to their intercourse, and takes away

all the grounds of jealousy and distrust that appeared insepar-
able from any other plan, and we are persuaded that, on deliberate examination, it will not be thought that these benefits
have been obtained by any material sacrifices on our part.
The number of men on the militia returns of the Lower Province in June, 1792, amounted to 37,446, which, on a very
moderate computation, may be considered as augmented to
40,000 by the 24th June, 1794, at which time the militia returns
of Upper Canada, amounted to 5,350 ; and we must further
consider the religious communities, the numerous parochial
clergy, and no less numerous practitioners of physic and law in
the Lower Province, as still increasing this disproportion, to
say nothing of the diminution of our numbers by the recruits engaged in the Provincial corps. We are aware that it
will be objected that the Indian trade, joined to our other
demands, consumes a much larger proportion of liquor than an
eighth. We are, however, induced to believe that the quantity so
consumed is overrated in the estimation of the public. Let it be
considered that the extensive settlements of Vermont are supplied with this article through Montreal, and that the fisheries
at Chaleur and Gaspe, and the canoeing and batteauing business, take off a large quantity for the people so employed, over
and above their ordinary consumption. Besides, from an attentive
examination and inquiry, it appeared to us that the same number
of inhabitants of Lower Canada consumed a far more considerable quantity of spirits, perhaps double, of what would be used by
an equal number in this Province. Instead of tea, so generally in
use among us, a glass of rum and a crust of bread is the usual
breakfast of the French Canadian. The rigour of their climate
is alleged as the cause of their having frequent recourse to it at
other times in the day, and their numerous holidays lead to

G

such habits of idleness and dissipation as are favourable to the consumption of rum. And let it also be considered that upon this plan we participate in the articles transported by the Ottawa River. But whatever doubt may exist with respect to this particular article, in every other that is likely to become liable to taxation our consumption will be far less than an eighth ; for besides the articles of this description that will enter into the very considerable trade which the Lower Province carries on with Vermont, the luxury of its towns will consume more than merely in proportion to the number of its inhabitants. While we were thus receiving a proportional share of the duties levied at Quebec, we considered it as no unreasonable concession on our parts to agree to suspend the exercise of our right to lay duties upon any articles coming into this country from Lower Canada, and thus to satisfy their Commissioners that while we were participating in the revenues collected by them, we would not embarrass their trade with any additional impositions. In thus resigning to them for a time the right to impose and levy duties for us, as well as for themselves, we had the best of all securities that this confidence would not be abused— namely, that they could do nothing to injure us that would not injure themselves much more. Besides, we were well assured before we consented to this Article, that such a sum was about to be raised as would afford for our part a sufficiency to defray our necessary expenditure. In a business so entirely new and untried, we judge it expedient to make the term of our agreement short, as the relative situation between the two Provinces may probably in a little time undergo such a change that regulations which would be highly reasonable and expedient might in a few years be inconvenient and improper, and under the expectation that the experience of a couple of years would enable us to rectify whatever may have been mistaken or over-looked in the present agreement.

All of which is most respectfully submitted, &c.

JOHN MUNRO.
JOHN McDOWELL.
RICHARD CARTWRIGHT.

To the Hon John Lees.

KINGSTON, 10th August, 1798.

DEAR SIR,—As we shall meet in a few months to discuss the subject of the provisional agreement between our respective Provinces, it may probably facilitate and forward the business to enter into some previous explanation, and indeed it is incumbent on us to account for our non-compliance with this agreement. Though individually I cannot send you anything formal or authentic, and my brother Commissioners are at too great a distance to be consulted, yet I have reason to believe that they will not disavow either my principles or facts, and indeed these appear too evident and conclusive to derive additional importance from any diplomatic sanction. Being, however, myself a convert (for you know my bias was originally the other way), I may possibly, like other converts, have too much zeal for my new opinions, and shall therefore be glad to receive any remarks or strictures on them from you or any of your colleagues previous to our personal conference. But to proceed to the question : Our rights to a portion of the duties collected at Quebec, under the authority of the Legislature of Lower Canada, arises from the plainest principles of equity, and is not derived from any positive stipulations between the two Provinces. This was so obvious, that the Act for laying such duties was immediately followed by one for appointing Commissioners to treat with Commissioners from this Province,

whose object was not to discuss this right, but to ascertain the
proportion of the duties justly applicable to each Province. This
was in the first instance adjusted agreeably to the respective
population of each, it being supposed to imply the same relative trade in, and consumption of, the dutiable articles, and at
the same time occasion was very properly taken to make such
regulations as would prevent the Legislatures of the two Provinces from clashing with each other in matters of revenue.
Before the expiration of the agreement under the first commission, the treaty with the United States of America took place,
which rendered this plain and simple criterion no longer proper or just, and it required a more complicated plan to ascertain the quantity of the dutiable articles consumed with us or
passing up the St. Lawrence for the purposes of trade ; but our
right to the amount of the duties on such articles, when ascertained, hath been unequivocally recognised under the Commissioners.   It rests, indeed, on the solid foundations' of justice
and candour ; and though the amount may be varied, the principle cannot be affected by the state of our intercourse with the
United States.   This being premised, I am equally ready to
declare that it results as an indisputable duty, from our political
relation as a dependency of the British Empire, to adopt and
enforce, as far as practicable, every regulation of trade that
may tend to employ British ships and enrich British subjects,
and exclude or discourage the interference of aliens.   On this
principle, and not on any idea of its being a *sine qua non* to our
receiving a share of the duties, we assented without hesitation
to the proposal made by the Commissioners of the Lower Province, that we should, agreeably to the power given us by the
Treaty, impose the same duties on articles coming into this
Province from the American States as they would be liable to

at the port of Quebec, and take measures for the collecting of them, *as far as our local circumstances would admit.* It was supposed at this time that the Government of the United States would on their parts have immediately proceeded to avail themselves of the power given them by this Treaty to check our intercourse with their territory, by making establishments at Detroit and elsewhere for collecting the Atlantic duties ; and yet it is evident, from the penning of the article, that difficulties respecting its being carried into effect were even then foreseen, but certainly not to the extent in which they prosecuted themselves when the measure came under the discussion of the Legislature, and when gentlemen assembled from every part of the Province could point out the facility with which every regulation might be eluded.   Indeed, when our geographical situation comes to be attentively considered, and the unlimited participation given to the citizens of America in the use of our portages, and in the navigation of the lakes and rivers which are common boundary between them and us for more than a thousand miles, it is not easy to point out how the collection of duties could be at all enforced ; and it will be readily agreed that it would require a much larger sum than the amount of all our revenues to support the establishments necessary for this purpose, and it would not only be absurd and ridiculous in the extreme to pass a law without providing for the execution of it, but in this case would be a fraud upon the Lower Province, by a compliance merely in words, and not in effect, with the article in question.   In a Bill for this purpose which made some progress in our Legislature, about sixteen places were fixed upon for the residence of custom-house officers, and even these were thought too few.   Another necessary consequence of such provisions must have been, to subject the trade of

Lower Canada with this country to all the expense, delay, and embarrassment of custom-house formalities, at every place of lading or unlading, whether in vessels or boats, or in carriages on the portages, in order to ascertain whether they were really what they were declared to be, and not a cloke for dutiable articles brought from the States. The effect of this upon the trade will be best understood by the commercial gentlemen of Montreal, who are so greatly and justly alarmed at a Bill brought into the Legislative Council of the then Province of Quebec in 1787, entitled "A Bill to explain and amend the Act entitled ' An Act or Ordinance for promoting the inland navigation.'" The declarations, manifests, and entries then contemplated were full as easy and simple as they could be admitted to be in the present case, and they were considered so harassing and vexatious as to call forth the united remonstrance of all the mercantile people concerned in the trade, in consequence of which they were very properly given up.

These considerations would of themselves, perhaps, be allowed to be sufficient to have made us pause, but they are at present the less necessary to be insisted upon, as, however weighty and important, they were not the predominant ones to induce our Legislature to postpone the ratification of the Provincial agreement, and to request a further conference with the Lower Province on that part of it which respects the imposition of duties on articles coming from the American States. In taking a view of the present state of our commercial intercourse with these States, I believe I am much within the bounds in asserting, that we annually send into their territory in the neighbourhood of Detroit, and towards the Illinois and Mississippi, to the amount of £60,000 sterling in articles of British manufacture ; wine, and the produce of our West Indian islands ;

all of which, according to the table of American duties, would be
liable to the exactions of from 25 to 50 cents per gallon on
spirits ; from 20 to 56 cents per gallon on wine ; 9 cents per lb·
on loaf sugar ; 5 cents per lb. on coffee ; 15 per cent. *ad valorem*
on arms, leather, and several articles ; 12½ per cent. on others ;
and not less than 10 per cent. on any. Compared with these,
our scale of duties is low indeed, limited at present to a very
few articles, and I presume will never be extended to British
manufactures, which greatly exceed in value all the other
articles which are used in this trade. What we receive from the
States is really almost nothing, and of that little but a part is
liable to pay duty. What is brought in is by adventurers who
can only be considered as mere peddlers ; even they seldom appear a second time, and no established mercantile house
among them, great or small, hath yet engaged in the trade of
this country. Let the mercantile gentlemen of Montreal say
whether, since the Treaty, the quantity of goods, even wines and
spirits not excepted, sent to Detroit and Machinac has not
rather increased than diminished. The demand for spirits
and sugar for our internal consumption, indeed, is probably
lessened, as the first has been in a considerable degree supplied
by our distillations from grain, and the latter from the domestic manufacture of maple sugar. But the imports of all kinds
for what may be called our foreign trade, if I may judge by the
quantity of goods that pass this place, are annually increasing,
and as the American settlements along the St. Lawrence and
the Lakes increase, will go on augmenting. The natural, I had
almost said the only outlet for all the produce of these settlements is by the St. Lawrence, whose waters are sufficient to
carry the largest rafts of lumber to your sea-ports, and this
lumber, which is itself a valuable article of commerce, may

at the same time be made a vehicle for transporting their wheat, flour, and potash to a market. This by the way of Oswego is utterly impossible, as besides going against the current, no raft could be got through Wood Creek, and there is moreover the land carriage from Schenectady to Albany Now, it is a matter of course to purchase our supplies where we sell our surplus produce, particularly when these supplies are to be had on as good terms and can be more easily transported than from other markets ; and the price of transport from Albany to Oswego is actually double the expense of that from Montreal to Kingston, and consequently to any place not more distant on the American shore. Such are the advantages we possess, which, co-operating with the high duties in the American ports, give us a superiority that we should be cautious of depriving ourselves of. Could the United States enforce the collection of their Atlantic duties on our inland commerce with them, they must necessarily operate as a bounty to take the trade from us, and turn it into their own channels; or at best we should have to pay a pound where we could collect a penny. It is therefore greatly to our own advantage, for the Lower Province in a still greater degree than for us, that the intercourse between us and the States should remain unrestrained. But it will be said that we have no security that the Government of America will allow it to remain so. This is true, and it is so much their interest that it should not, that they have probably been passive on the occasion, only from the difficulty and expense of enforcing revenue laws under the circumstances we are placed in with regard to each other. But as we must lose more than we can well calculate should they make the experiment, it does not seem consistent with common prudence for us, by first adopting the measure, to provoke them to it, for we cannot suppose that they would be slow in attempting to retaliate.

From this view of the subject, which has presented itself in the course of the lengthy and deliberate discussion which it has undergone in our Legislature, and which, though perhaps not the most obvious, is the true point in which it ought to be regarded, the Lower Province will see that it is not because we are unwilling to concur with them in any necessary or useful regulations of trade, or from any partial or selfish motives, that we have not proceeded to confirm in its fullest extent the Provincial agreement entered into in January, 1797, but because our compliance appeared likely to produce the very evils it was intended to guard against, and instead of operating to establish and promote trade in the hands of British subjects, to have a direct tendency to make it of less value to them, and to encourage aliens to supplant them in a very valuable and growing branch of it. Indeed, their very liberal conduct in voting us our proportion of the duties last year, previous to any formal reconsideration of the agreement, leaves us no reason to doubt of their candour in the prosecution of the business, and of their willingness to concur in such modifications as shall appear best calculated to meet the exigencies of the case. For my part, I. am impressed with the fullest conviction that they will deprecate rather than urge us to begin a war of revenue regulations with the United States, by which they may lose a great deal and can certainly gain very little.

To this lengthy epistle about matters of public concern, permit me to add assurances of my personal regard and esteem.

J am, &c.,

RICHARD CARTWRIGHT.

To J. McGill, Esq.

KINGSTON, 31st Dec., 1801.

MY DEAR SIR,—I hope your Legislature will not be too much in haste to multiply duties upon imports, for though I do not consider them as any breach of the Treaty with the Americans, to whom they will still leave all their relative advantages, they will bear hard upon this Province, who, from the nature of their returns, which consist chiefly in bulky articles, can have little direct intercourse with the United States. For my part, I have never had a single article from thence, and the duty on tobacco, as far as I am concerned, may be considered a duty on British manufacture rather than an article of trade with America. I am, however, very ready to abandon this and tea to the discretion of your Legislature ; but iron and leather are articles of such general and indispensable necessity as should induce the Legislature to give every encouragement to render them plenty and cheap. Such evidently is the interest of the public, and the manufacture of leather at L'Assumption, and of iron at Bastican and St. Maurice, are certainly not of that importance as to warrant them in levying a contribution of ten per cent. on the consumption of these Provinces for their support, whatever Messrs. Craigie, Coffin, Bell, and Badgley may say to the contrary. In addition to the articles of the peace which you mention, I understand that Portugal, Naples, and Turkey remain as before the war. I should certainly have rejoiced at any further acquisitions that Great Britain had retained, but however highly we may be disposed to rate her strength and resources (and they have in this struggle been displayed to an extent that would heretofore have been deemed romantic), on a cool consideration of circumstances, I think it will be agreed that the present peace has in no degree blasted her laurels.

R. C.

CHAPTER VIII.

SESSION OF 1801—ELECTION OF SPEAKER—DISPUTED ELECTION—
APPROPRIATIONS—BOUNTY ON HEMP—LETTER TO REV. J.
STRACHAN—GRANT FOR ROADS—GRANT FOR PURCHASE OF HEMP—
ALIEN ACT—DESERTION ACT—LETTER TO CHIEF JUSTICE ALCOCK—
CONDUCT OF MR. THORPE—DUTY ON TEA ON HAWKERS—ESTABLISH-
MENT OF DISTRICT SCHOOLS—LETTER SUPPOSED TO BE WRITTEN BY
LIEUTENANT-GOVERNOR—MR. THORPE SENT TO SIERRA LEONE—
CHARACTER OF ATTORNEY-GENERAL.

MEMORANDUM OF TRANSACTIONS IN FIRST SESSION OF THE
THIRD PROVINCIAL PARLIAMENT OF UPPER CANADA.

THE election of a Speaker gave rise to considerable intrigue.
Some part of the private conduct of D. W. Smith, Esq., which
was supposed to have occasioned the fall of the late Attorney-
General, and to have produced other breaches in the society
at York, was made use of with such success that he who had
been unanimously called to the chair on a former occasion, had
now the majority of but a single voice. Three members, however, who would have voted for him, did not arrive till the
election was over. The session began with a considerable degree of warmth in the House of Assembly respecting the appointment of a new Clerk to that House. On some controversy between the emigrant French general, Count de Puisaye
and Mr. Angus McDonell, which had been examined before a
Committee of Council in the month of August, the Committee,
in their report to the Governor, had declared Mr. Mc-

Donell's conduct to have been such as to render him unworthy
of any office under the Government. The Governor hereupon
signified to Mr. McDonell that he was no longer Clerk to the
House of Assembly, and appointed a Mr. McLean in his stead.
At the meeting of the Assembly both Clerks took their seats at
the table, Mr. McLean by virtue of his recent commission
from the Governor, which was the only notice the House had
of his appointment, and Mr. McDonell under his old commission, which he contended could not be set aside without the
consent of the House.   In these pretensions he was warmly
supported by several members, and it was not till after some
days spent in the controversy that the point was given up : yet
the House did not allow Mr. McDonell to retire without passing a vote which expressed their approbation of his conduct, and thanked him for his diligence in the discharge of
the duties of the office he had filled.   That the appointment
rests in the Governor is without dispute ; yet, in filling it, some
regard should be had to the body under which it is to be exercised, and it is probable that had the Governor signified by
a message to the House that he could not with propriety allow
Mr. McDonell to hold his office, and had therefore appointed
another, which was an act of civility they had a right to expect, in all probability there would have been an immediate
and silent acquiescence. The House of Assembly were next
occupied in settling the mode of proceeding on a petition of
the inhabitants of York and Northumberland respecting a disputed election, and examining into the merits of the petition.
The result was that Mr. Justice Alcock, the sitting member,
was declared not duly elected, and the election itself void.   It
appeared in evidence that very unwarrantable steps had been
taken by the friends of Mr. Alcock to procure him to be re-

turned. A large majority of the electors were evidently
against him ; but while those on his side were giving him votes,
a drunken man of the opposite party was ordered to be taken
into the custody of a constable for some noisy behaviour which,
on such an occasion, might very well have been passed over.
This act of authority gave such offence to some of the bystand-
ers that they interposed themselves between him and the officer
after he had been arrested, by which means the man made
his escape in the crowd. While this was doing, two or three
people were hastily called up to vote for Mr. Alcock, which gave
him a small majority ; and hereupon a Mr. Weeks, an Irish
lawyer, the Judge's most active agent, cried out, " A riot ! a
riot ! " and prevailed with the returning officer to close the poll.
During the whole of this investigation, Mr. Alcock behaved in
a most extraordinary manner, being constantly present in the
House and taking notes, but pertinaciously declining to reply
to the attorney for the petitioners, or to enter at all upon a
vindication of his election. Before the House had come to a
determination, he handed to some of the members, while the
House was sitting, a paper, drawn up by his friend the Attorney-General, stating doubts of the competency of the House to
decide the case, as no law had been enacted in the Province relative to this subject, and the law that regulated such proceedings in England being wholly inapplicable here from the
paucity of members, and concluding with the insinuation that
the Governor might very probably not agree to the issuing
another writ. When all the evidence had been gone through,
and the result was to be determined upon, Mr. Alcock was, at
the request of the House, desired by the Speaker to withdraw ;
but he replied that " he was still a member of that House,
and would not withdraw unless they threw him out *neck and*

heels," and he actually kept his seat while the resolutions respecting himself were determining. Such conduct requires no
comment. It is allowed that some of the members had, individually, little claim to respectability, and that some others
held doctrines respecting the extent of their authority that no
reasonable man would subscribe to ; yet, as a public body, they
have, unquestionably, a claim to at least the appearance of respect, and when this is so glaringly withheld by persons high
in office, it tends evidently to excite opposition against the
Government itself, and to raise an idea that they, wish to control, in an authoritative manner, the freedom of their deliberations. It seems hardly proper for a Judge of the Court of
King's Bench to become a candidate for a seat in a popular
Assembly. The usual mode of canvassing for such a situation
but little accords with the gravity and dignity expected in such
a character, and it might be feared that in the administration
of criminal law he would not be altogether unbaissed should
any of his opponents be convicted before him in cases where
the penalty is undefined and left to the discretion of the
Judge. But there seemed to be a peculiar degree of indecorum
in a person of this description taking his seat in the House of
Assembly under a return which had been obtained by the most
glaring violation of law. While these transactions were going on in the House of Assembly, some attempts were made
there to repeal so much of an Act passed in the 4th session of
the second Provincial Parliament, entitled "An Act for the more
equal representation of the Commons of the Province in Parliament, and for the better defining the qualification of electors," as made a previous residence of seven years in the
Province a necessary qualification for an elector, and also to
abolish the mode of summary convictions before the magistrates

for selling of spirits, &c., without license, under pretence of its being a dangerous encroachment on the privilege of trial by jury; but these attempts proved ineffectual, and were rejected by a considerable majority of the House. The measure that was first passed in that House, and brought up to the Council in the shape of a Bill, was for paying the wages of the members of the Assembly out of the Provincial fund ; and because that Bill was rejected by the Council, they were so highly offended that some of the most violent had nearly prevailed upon the majority of the House to do no more business ; and although they did not succeed to the extent of their wishes, yet they prevailed so far as to procure their concurrence to an attempt to force the Council to a compliance with this selfish measure, by tacking it to the Bill for ratifying the provisional agreement with Lower Canada relating to duties, &c. But this attempt being unanimously repulsed by that body with proper steadiness, though without asperity, as calculated to infringe the constitutional freedom of their deliberations, another fit of ill-humour succeeded ; and it was not without allowing some time for this to subside, and using a considerable degree of management, that a majority of three could be procured to prevent the public business from being wholly impeded. With this feeble majority the provisional agreement with the Lower Province was carried through, as well as the necessary measures consequent thereto of establishing ports of entry and proper officers for collecting, on articles coming into this Province from the United States, the same duties that are payable at Quebec. The business of appropriating the money in the hands of the Receiver-General, arising from various funds, which had till General Hunter's administration been done simply by a vote of the House of Assembly, was also put

upon a proper footing by a Bill specifying the different items
of expenditure.   And though these articles were again inserted
which had been struck out by the Council in the last session
of the preceding Parliament as amendments, and which occasioned the different branches of the Legislature to separate in
very ill humour, that body had recovered sufficient temper
and moderation to give them no opposition on the present occasion.   The reasons which induced the Legislative Council
not to accede to the wishes of the Assembly in changing the
mode of paying their allowance of 10s. per diem, which they
now receive by a direct assessment on their constituents, to a
charge on the general revenue, were that this sum, if taken
from the Provincial fund, would require to be replaced by
some other tax, at which the public, as is generally the case
on the imposition of any new tax, would be dissatisfied and
pay it with reluctance ; whereas they were reconciled by long
usage to the one at present applied to this purpose.   Besides,
it appeared highly probable that could the members of the
Assembly take their allowance immediately from the Provincial treasury, they might be less inclined to dispatch than to
protract business ; the temptation to which was much weaker
at present, as their payment was attended with some delay,
and being immediately felt by their constituents, they would
be cautious of any unnecessary augmentation.   The plan of
allowing wages to any branch of the Legislature seems to be
reprehensible under any form.   The honour of such a situation
ought to be considered as a sufficient compensation, and persons who, from circumstances of fortune and education, can be
influenced by such motives, are likely to discharge their duty
better than the needy and the ignorant, with whom, perhaps,
the allowance is the principal object, and who are often the

favourites of a majority of the electors, though generally incapable of understanding the tendency of public measures, and liable consequently to be influenced, by artful management, to support, alike such as may be either factious or oppressive. The only remedy left for this evil is, that as the electors now feel immediately the burden of paying their representatives, they may be induced to prefer those who would decline any pecuniary compensation. The Council would therefore have ill discharged their duty were they to have given up a point so beneficial in its tendency, and which would have been lost for ever by yielding to the wishes of the Assemby, which proceeded evidently from motives of mere personal advantage to the individuals who composed it. During these proceedings a new writ was issued for the Counties of York and Northumberland, and Mr. Angus McDonell, the late Clerk of the House of Assembly, was elected by a large majority, and took his seat as a member. Mr. Alcock declined becoming a candidate on this occasion, yet the people, whose zeal was occasionally heightened by the effect of ardent spirits during this exercise of their sovereign authority, showed a strong disposition at intervals to insult him and his friends.

Two days before the time at which it was generally understood that the business of the session was to close, a Bill passed the Assembly to encourage the growth of hemp by a bounty, but so loosely drawn up as to make it necessary for the Council to new-model it entirely. On returning it thus altered to the Assembly, it was rejected under the pretence of its being a Money Bill, in which it was trenching upon their privileges for the Council to make alterations, and they passed a vote authorizing the Lieutenant-Governor to expend several hundred pounds in bounties, and for the purchase of seed, at his discre-

II

tion. Though the present Governor had hitherto constantly refused to advance money upon a vote of the House, and insisted that this could only be done by a legislative act, yet in this instance he seemed to have abandoned his own principles; for under sanction of this vote he appointed, by proclamation, commissioners to dispose of this money for the purpose therein expressed. Influenced by a favourite measure that had also been pressed upon him by His Majesty's Ministers, he perhaps overlooked the inconsistency of his conduct, and the improper weight he was giving to the democratic branch, by now countenancing their former pretensions, and thus encouraging them again to regard the Council, in money matters, as mere cyphers. Probably he might have thought himself at liberty to act in this manner from a knowledge that the Council were full as much disposed as the Assembly to promote the object in view. But in matters of legislation and government nothing should be assumed as the will and intention of any public body, in the exercise of such functions, that is not sanctioned by its formal and official act. It was the general wish of the Legislature to make the Court of King's Bench more easily accessible, and an Act was passed to allow all proceedings preparatory to the trial, and previous to judgment and execution, to be transacted in the office of the Clerk of the Crown, which was erected in each District of the Province. Another Act on the subject of holding to bail also passed both Houses.

As it was the intention of the Legislature not to allow of imprisonment for debt except in cases of meditated fraud by leaving the Province, which the plaintiff was to avow his suspicion of upon oath, they considered that such fraud should be a sufficient ground for arrest in all cases, however small the amount, and that to carry this into effect it was necessary to authorize the Justices of the Peace, upon oath made before them of suspicion of such meditated fraud, to grant a warrant for the temporary detention of the party till the regular process of the Clerk's office could be obtained, and detention in no case to exceed eight days. This last provision was, however, so carelessly worded, that upon strict construction it was considered to extend only to cases where a suit had been previously commenced, and the former, by a very arbitrary construction of the Court of King's Bench, in the face as well of the spirit as the letter of the Act, was made to extend only to sums above £10 sterling. To explain these, and to prevent all possibility of misconstruction for the future, was the sole purport of the Act in question; but though brought into the House of Assembly by the Solicitor-General, and supported and amended in the Council by the Chief Justice, the Governor refused his assent to it. It was but too evident that he was influenced in this, as well as in some other measures, by Mr. Justice Alcock, seconded by the Attorney-General, his most obsequious friend; and it was equally notorious that Mr. Alcock was so much at enmity with the Chief Justice that the support of any measure by the latter was sufficient to draw upon it the hostility of the former, who was, besides, determined to resist every departure from the established rules of English practice. It seems not very consistent with the sound understanding usually displayed by our Governor to allow any man to have so much his ear as to lead him to oppose the wishes of the other branches of the Legislature in measures from which no ill consequences could possibly follow, and which were merely explanatory of a former law; and it may be regarded as a singularity that a man bred to the profession of a soldier should appear to have so much reverence for the intricacies of legal chicanery. A Bill was carried through the House of Assembly to prevent lands from being taken in execution, and declaring that they should be no otherwise liable for debt than they were in England. This Bill was rejected by the Council, who, in consequence thereof, passed another, which was concurred in by the Assembly, " to regulate the sale of lands taken in execution," wherein it was directed that personal chattels should be sold in the first instance, and resort had to the land only in cases where these were insufficient for the discharge of the debt, and that they should in no case be sold till a year after they had been seized and advertised by the Sheriff. This Bill was reserved by the Governor for His Majesty's pleasure, merely because it appeared, as he expressed himself in private conversation, " to confirm by a side wind the decision of the Court of King's Bench." The decision here referred to was, that lands in this Province were liable to be seized and sold in execution for debt, in which Mr. Alcock had dissented from the other two judges, and which it was understood would be put in train for being appealed to the King in Council for their final determination. The promoters of the · Bill, however, had no such view, nor could the Bill in candour be so considered ; it contained no declaratory clause upon the subject, but left the question where it found it, and was merely calculated to remedy the inconvenience complained of by a majority of the Assembly, that lands might be seized and sold with such a rapidity as to afford little hope of its yielding more than a small part of its value.

Whatever may be the final determination of this question, it appears but just that a man's property of every description should be liable to the payment of his debts. It is not only more consonant to our notions of equity, but in my opinion more agreeable to sound policy, than to shut him up in a prison, by which his labour is lost to society, and his family often reduced to the utmost distress ; and as this imprisonment has no other limitation than the will of the creditor, or an occasional Insolvent Act, he is frequently made to suffer for his indiscretion, or perhaps misfortune, a severer punishment than the law inflicts on many crimes. In other instances, again, the profligate wretch lives in luxury within the limits of his confinement, while the law has placed his property out of the reach of his creditors. The mode pointed out in England of levying a third part of the yearly value of an estate cannot apply here, where lands are yet but in the first stage of cultivation, and where all being proprietors, it would not, at all events, be easy to find lessees for an improved farm. Yet even in England real property is sold in cases of bankruptcy, and recently to satisfy debts due to Government ; and why the principle of the bankruptcy laws should not in this particular be applied to all other cases, no reason could probably be assigned that would appear valid to those who have not been in the habit of respecting precedent more than justice. A Bill brought in by the Chief Justice for enabling married women to alienate landed property without levying a fine, also passed both Houses; this, while it retained the practice of private examination, to prevent a surprise upon the party and to make her sensible of the sacrifice she was about to make, retrenched such forms as tended only to create expense, and which, under the peculiar situation of this Province, would be productive of great embarrassment. This Bill, however, was reserved for His Majesty's pleasure, and, with others formerly sent home under the same circumstances, will probably be heard of no more. His Majesty's Ministers have matters of more importance to attend to than investigate nicely those comparatively so minute, and are, besides, not likely to be in haste to sanction measures the propriety of which seemed to be doubtful to their agent upon the spot, to whose control they were constitutionally committed. A Bill to define what should be deemed and taken to be public roads throughout this Province was rejected by the Governor, it having been omitted therein expressly to except the rights of the Crown. These were the only things worthy of notice that passed during this session, which began on the 28th of May and ended the 9th day of July, 1801. In the meantime very rapid progress was making in passing the patents for lands which had hitherto been very much neglected, to the great disgust of the people. This neglect was in part owing to the subject itself, which, from the lapse of time, was involved in some difficulty ; but much more to the indolence, ignorance and perverseness of the officers employed in the principal departments through which they must pass, of whom scarcely one seemed to possess either talents or inclination for business except the Surveyor-General, whose diligence was always exemplary, and to whose methodical correctness the Province is much indebted. The zeal of the Governor in urging this business was well seconded by the Attorney-General, who seems to be as diligent and regular as his predecessor was indolent and incorrect.

To the Rev. J. Strachan.

March 17th, 1804.

DEAR SIR,—The late session of our Legislature will, I think, be found to have been useful to the public, and, consequently, honourable to the members. They have passed an Act for appropriating £1,000 towards opening and repairing the public roads. As it was foreseen that, from local attachments and partialities, it would be difficult for the members of the Council and Assembly to agree in opinion respecting the distribution of this sum, in order to avoid this source of discord, which might probably have proved fatal to the measure, it was prudently left with the Governor and Executive Council to appoint Commissioners to lay out the money in such places as they should deem most generally useful. By another Act, the sum of £400 has been appropriated annually towards the erecting of public buildings in the town of York, for the accommodation of the Legislative Council and House of Assembly, the Executive Council, the Courts of Justice, and the several public offices of the Province. By another Act, a sum (about £190) has been appropriated for purchasing a set of the Statutes of the British Parliament for each of the several districts of the Province. Under a former Act the sum of £300 had been annually appropriated for printing the laws and journals, and the latter, with the merits of which you are acquainted, have actually cost the Province £800. The House of Assembly, sensible at last of this waste of public money, passed a Bill for applying on the present occasion this sum of £300 for printing a complete edition of all the Provincial Statutes, including those of the present session, to be distributed for the information of the public, and reserving the sum of £80 for the printing of the laws in future, and left the remaining £220 to be disposed of hereafter as the Legislature should think proper. From such a Bill you will naturally conclude that the other branches of the Legislature would not withhold their assent, and I think it likely that better use will hereafter be made of the money than publishing the Journals of the Assembly, which are about as useful and entertaining as the log-book of a ship. It was also thought ex-

pedient to hold out some further encouragement for the cultivation of hemp, and it was agreed on all hands that the most
successful expedient for this purpose would be to put it in the
power of the cultivator to obtain on the spot a reasonable
price in ready money.   This the scarcity of mercantile capital
in the country left no room to expect without legislative aid.
An Act was therefore passed to authorize the Governor to apply the sum of £1,000, together with the further sum of about
£400 remaining of a former grant, for paying a bounty on the
growth and exportation of hemp, to purchase hemp at £40 per
ton.   This money is to be laid out by Commissioners to be
appointed in different parts of the Province, and it is supposed
will be fully equal to the purchase of all the hemp that has
been raised.   This is to be shipped under the direction of the
Commissioners, and the proceeds returned to the Provincial
Treasury, so that the Province is not likely to lose by the measure even in a pecuniary point of view.   In the meantime, the
cultivation of the article will be more generally attended to,
and the Government at home, it is hoped, will take the hint
and adopt some similar plan for purchasing the hemp of the
country, without which the business will infallibly languish;
though under such an arrangement it would probably be pushed
to considerable extent, and be of much benefit to the Province,
particularly to the western parts of it, where the soil and
climate appear best adapted to the growth of the article, and
the remote situation of which must prevent them from exporting wheat, flour, &c.   Government, through the medium of
their Commissary and Naval Departments, might purchase and
send it to England without any, or at very little, extra expense.
The renewal of the war with France having been mentioned in
the Governor's speech, and the necessity thence inferred of

guarding the internal tranquillity of the Province against the insidious attempts of secret enemies, the subject was considered with the attention that so weighty a matter deserved. In the course of the investigation it was understood that the Executive Government already possessed sufficient power of coercion and restraint over alien enemies ; but it appeared likely that other instruments might be employed, and some upon whom it would be difficult to fix the proposed discriminating term of alien. It was agreed also, that every political society ought to possess the power of excluding from its limits all strangers who evinced a disposition to excite dissensions and inflame discontents among its respective orders ; or, in other words, to disturb the established government thereof; and on this principle a law was framed, authorizing persons in certain public situations—namely, the Governor, members of the Legis lative and Executive Council, Judges of the Court of King's Bench, and others, to be commissioned by the Governor— on complaint being made against any person not a stated resident in the Province (that is, who had not been an inhabitant for six months before, and had not taken the oath of allegiance), to call such person before them and require him to give an account of himself; and if he appeared to have been guilty of improper conduct in this respect, or to have given just cause of suspicion of having sinister views of this kind, to order him out of the Province, or to make him find sureties for his good behaviour while remaining therein, and the necessary provisions were added for enforcing obedience to such orders. An Act has also passed for the more exemplary punishment of persons enticing soldiers to desert, and of those who harbour or conceal deserters. The peculiar circumstances of this country required a law of this kind, and it does little more than authorize the detention of persons charged with such offences, by a warrant from a magistrate, till they can be tried before the Judge of Assize or Court of King's Bench, and if found guilty by a jury, they are to suffer six months' imprisonment, and in very flagrant cases a fine of £40 besides, and in case of inability to discharge the fine, public whipping. This punishment is little different from what is already inflicted by the English statute law; and the principal advantage of the Provincial law is, that it no longer leaves a doubt whether the provisions of the English law extended to this Province, and takes away the hope of escape from the offender, who might otherwise brave the law, and till the very moment of conviction withdraw beyond its reach. These are the matters of chief importance upon which the Legislature were employed, and it will be readily granted that they must have been tolerably diligent to have brought them to a close in a short session of four or five weeks. It is hardly necessary to take notice of Mr. Washburn's extravagant project for making Quebec a free port, or the zealous attempt of Mr. Rogers and a few others, in order probably to secure their re-election, to repeal the law which makes a residence of seven years in the Province neces-sary, before any person who does not come immediately from some other part of His Majesty's dominions can legally vote for a member of the House of Assembly, as they were both re-jected in the Assembly itself. The Legislature were convened on the 1st of February, but there was not a quorum of the Assembly till the 8th; they were prorogued on the 9th of March. This will be their last session, as there must be a new election in July next, the present members of the House of Assembly having there continued for four years.

R. C.

To the Hon. Chief Justice Alcock.

KINGSTON, 14th March, 1807.

DEAR SIR,—Our Session of Parliament hath terminated in a manner the most desirable to the friends of good order, and the most mortifying to Mr. Thorpe, who has been completely foiled in his attempts to do mischief. The House of Assembly, by their late conduct, have made amends for the improprieties of the preceding session. Mr. Thorpe endeavoured to persuade them that the duties levied under Acts of the British Parliament were at the disposal of the Provincial Legislature, and that this Province was entitled to a proportion of such of those duties as were received at the port of Quebec, in the same manner as it was to a proportion of those levied under the authority of the Legislature of Lower Canada ; and they were sufficiently inclined to listen to a doctrine which would place a large additional sum of money at their disposal. But after attentively considering the 31st of the King, they, to a man, saw the absurdity of such a pretension, and gave up the point. Driven from this broad ground, he then insisted that the duties imposed by the 14th of the King, on licenses for re-tailing spirits, were certainly at their disposal, and had actually been appropriated by a Provincial statute passed in the 33rd year of His Majesty's reign ; but it was contended that the words of this statute would not bear the construction which the Judge laboured to give it, and that the constant usage ever since showed that in passing that law the Legislature had no such object in contemplation ; or, granting him both these points, it was shown that by the 31st of the King the Provincial Legislature had not the power, if they had the intention, to do so. He was here again left alone, notwithstanding his pathetic exclamation, that " if they gave up this they gave up their freedom," and his almost treasonable allusions to the American revolution, produced, as he said, by parliamentary taxation. The only one of his factious measures on which there was a close division was a motion for an address respecting the U. E. Loyalists and military claimants, couched in insidious and inflammatory language,and which, being on a popular subject, he prevailed on Nelles, Washburn, Howard, Dorland, and a few others of equal capacity to support, and his motion was negatived by a majority of one only. On a question respecting the appointment of trustees to schools, he declaimed most vehemently against their being made Government jobs, and insisted that as five was to be the number, the House of Assembly should appoint three and the Legislative Council two ; but here he had only Mr. Clinch and Mr. Rogers on his side. You know the clamour raised by Mr. Weeks about a sum of money charged, very improperly we must allow, against the Provincial Fund, but on the order of General Hunter, without the concurrence of the other branches of the Legislature. This the Governor ordered to be replaced, and mentioned it in his speech. The House of Assembly, to show that it was not the money, but the principle, they had been contending for, on the 7th inst., passed a resolution to give back the money, and presented a handsome address to the Governor, expressing themselves satisfied that it had been expended for the benefit of the Province. On this occasion Mr. Thorpe was almost furious ; he accused them of sacrificing their freedom, giving up their constitution, &c. But in vain he declaimed and raved ; everybody but himself declared in favour of the resolution and address. It is impossible for me to speak of this man's conduct without indignation and contempt ; but our friend the Chief Justice has so much of the milk of human kindness in his disposition, that neither the personal indignities which he has received from Mr. Thorpe and his family, nor his political conduct, have been sufficient to rouse him into anything like hostility. Indeed, his tameness and condescension with respect to him are almost criminal in a person in his situation, besides being derogatory to his dignity. He endeavours, too, to persuade the Governor that as long as Mr. Thorpe does not act corruptly as a Judge, the other parts of his conduct are not sufficient grounds for suspending him. I have strenuously combated this doctrine, and insisted that he ought to have been suspended the moment his answer to the London address appeared ; but as that was not done, that his conduct in the House of Assembly would justly warrant this step as soon as the Legislature should be prorogued. The Governor, however, seems inclined to wait till he hears from home, in the hope that he will be recalled, as he wishes, in common with every good subject, that the Province should be rid of him ; and Mr. Thorpe, it seems, has expressed himself as if he were indifferent about holding his situation as a Judge, alleging that he could make more by practising as a lawyer in this country.

You see that I write you with the utmost freedom ; but I should not, perhaps, have entered so minutely into all these matters had not the Governor requested me to give you a par_ ticular account of our transactions, as he has not leisure to write himself. I left York on the 8th, and the Legislature was to be prorogued on the 10th. The business of the session was considered as finished when I came away. We have passed a law imposing the additional duties on teas, &c., laid by the Legislature of Lower Canada two years ago, for the purpose of building their gaols, solely, however, on the principle of expediency, and from a wish to preserve a good understanding be-

tween the two Provinces, and in full confidence that the duties
upon such of these articles as have passed Coteau du Lac since
the operation of the above-mentioned law will be accounted
for to this Province. If it be said that this ought not to be
done, except from the time in which we co-operated in this
measure, I consider it in the first place as a matter of right, and
independent of any stipulation, that we are entitled to a drawback on everything consumed within the Province ; and, at all
events, we could not, without degrading ourselves, take up the
measure till it had been formally announced by your Government to ours, which it never was till late in the last year. We
have also passed a law imposing a duty on licenses to hawkers,
peddlers, etc., and one for establishing a school in every district which gives £100 per annum to the master of each such
school, who is to be selected by trustees nominated by the
Lieut.-Governor, with a power in the latter to approve or re-
ject the person they recommend. It expires in four years if
not renewed, and this circumstance will probably very much
lessen its good effects. These, and the law which modifies and
renews our laws for imposing and levying rates and assessments in each district, are the only ones of material importance that have been passed. A Bill was brought in by Mr.
Sherwood, to repeal the law for establishing courts of justice and regulating their proceedings, and to introduce a new
system in its stead. That you may have a perfect idea of his
plan, I enclose you a copy of the Bill, which has been printed,
and which, by common consent, is to lie over till the next session. That our present system is not well adapted to the situation of the Province, we all feel ; but a single Judge invested
with all the powers of the Court of King's Bench, Common
Pleas and Exchequer, would be a bold innovation, and there

are other parts of the scheme that I have very strong objections to. If you could find leisure to communicate to me your opinion upon it, I should esteem it a particular favour. I believe the Legislature would be very ready to supply the expense of any establishment that might be necessary to make our judicial system more applicable to our geographical situation. I fear I have trespassed upon your patience, but I am disposed to consider you as still interested in what is passing amongst us, and, on that account, anxious that you should not be informed by halves.

The following letter may be supposed to have been written by the Lieutenant-Governor immediately after the prorogation of the Legislature in March, 1809 :—

The removal of Mr. Thorpe has unquestionably relieved the Government of the Province from an active and indefatigable instrument of mischief; yet his friends here boast of his appointment at Sierra Leone as an unequivocal proof of the approbation of his conduct by His Majesty's Ministers ; and this view of the subject is industriously obtruded upon the public, through the press of Mr. Wilcox, his bosom friend and most zealous partizan. The effects of his residence in this Province, however, will long be felt; for although we no longer hear the Government abused from the Bench by one of His Majesty's Judges, yet his example has given a degree of audacity to the factions that they would otherwise never have assumed. One of the most prominent characters among these is the before mentioned Mr. Wilcox, the printer, who, although once imprisoned by the House of Assembly for a libel on the majority of that House, and prosecuted, by the advice of the Attorney-General, for a most impudent libel on myself, still persists in attempting, by the grossest misrepresentations, to lessen the confidence of the people in the Government. In the prosecution for a libel, though its application was so pointed that its drift could not have been more clearly understood had my name been inserted at full length, he was acquitted ; and such is the disposition of some of the people of this Province, that he has been returned a member of the House of Assembly for one of the Counties without opposition. It is, indeed, much to be regretted that while every demagogue has a probable chance of obtaining a seat in that House, the Government have it not in their power to return a single member. This is owing to a want of proper foresight and precaution on the part of the late General Simcoe, who, on entering upon his administration, had it in his power to have made such arrangements with regard to the representation of the Province as might have always ensured the return of one of the Law Officers of the Crown to that House, which would have given great facility in conducting the business of the House, without affording any ground of complaint of undue influence on the part of the Governor. But such opportunity having been once lost will never be recovered, as the 34th of the King directs all subse-quent arrangements to be made by the Provincial Legislature. During the session of 1808, a circumstance took place unpre-cedented, I believe, in any legislative body. On a question that arose in the House of Assembly respecting some modification of a law for establishing schools, three of Mr. Thorpe's friends, who were opposed to the majority of the House, were deter-mined, at all events, to carry their point, and rather put a stop to all the business of the session than submit to the determi-nation of the majority. With this view, when the question was about to be put, they withdrew from the House, leaving it without a quorum, and immediately set off for their respective homes, which were at a very considerable distance. This happened near the close of the session, and after several of the members had obtained leave of absence. Some of these it became necessary to recall in order to give efficiency to the business that had actually been finished by the two Houses, and this could not be done till after an interval of several days. I thought it my duty to show the sense I entertained of the extraordinary conduct of these refractory members by taking from them some appointments they held under Government, and their conduct would of course be reprobated by every sensible man. These, however, are, unfortunately, not everywhere the majority, and the gentlemen in question have been returned to the present Parliament, in which they seem determined to be as troublesome as possible. Amidst all these perplexities, however, several measures of importance to the prosperity of the Province have been accomplished. The education of youth hath been provided for on a liberal scale; considerable sums of money have been obtained for improving the public roads; the culture of hemp hath been liberally encouraged, and collision with the Legislature of Lower Canada on the subject of revenue hath been avoided. I have also been able to obtain such a modification of the Militia Law, as abolishes the Lieutenancies in Counties, which were not only inapplicable to the circumstances of the Province, from the want of characters sufficiently distinguished to fill them, but by interposing the person in that situation to commission the officers, and issue all orders in their respective Counties, kept the Governor too much out of sight. The Legislative Council, originally nine in number, is now reduced to five members, including the Speaker, whose attendance can be relied on. Mr. Grant's age and infirmities and his distant residence render it impracticable for him to attend at the season when

I

the Legislature is usually convened, and Mr. Duncan hath vacated his seat, he residing in a foreign State beyond the term prescribed by law. It has therefore become necessary to appoint some new members, in order to give this body, which forms so useful a counterpoise to the rashness of the House of Assembly, its proper weight and influence. To recommend the persons who may occur to me as best qualified for this purpose will be the subject of another letter. I had flattered myself that in the Attorney-General I should have found an able and faithful adviser, and that his conduct would have added strength and respectability to the Government, but in this I have been most miserably disappointed. He not only has the most ungovernable temper that ever man was cursed with, but is withal self-sufficient, mercenary and rapacious. I give you the following as one among many instances of his indiscretion. In the session of the Legislature that was held in Feb., 1808, a Bill was introduced into the House of Assembly to alter the present mode of administering justice in civil cases by establishing in each district Courts of concurrent jurisdiction with the King's Bench in such cases. Without waiting to see what was likely to be the fate of the Bill, or what shape it would assume in its progress, he immediately presented a petition to the House, in his capacity of Attorney-General, requiring to be heard at their bar against the Bill, and this not only without my concurrence, but contrary to my remonstrances and even injunctions. His petition was treated, as might have been expected, with contempt; but it was not easy to remove the impression which it gave rise to, that this egregious piece of folly of Mr. Firth was a measure of the Government. As for the Bill in question it came to nothing. Instead of setting an example to the rest of the bar, of decent language and demeanour in Court, and a proper respect for the Bench, he indulges in the most intemperate sallies and insolent abuse against his opponents, and has on this account been more than once involved in very serious personal difficulties. Should the Bench not concur with him in his opinions, which are full as often wrong as right, he does not abstain from the most indecent reflections, exclaiming that he has no chance of obtaining justice, and uttering other insinuations equally improper and disrespectful to the Judges.   Nothing, indeed, has withheld them from making the strongest representations to me, in form, of his improper conduct, but the fear lest His Majesty's Ministers, from the frequency of my complaints against the public officers they send to the Colony, should form an opinion that I was improperly hard, harsh and unreasonably difficult in the article of their behaviour.   His accounts are swelled with charges unknown in those of his predecessors, and though these are, of course, struck out at the audit, yet they evince a disposition not very creditable to the character of any man, and might, without any great breach of charity, lead one to suspect that it might induce the person in question to avail himself of his official position to multiply prosecutions with a view to his own emolument.   From this sketch, which is very far from exaggeration, you will readily believe that instead of leaning upon him for support, or recurring to him for advice, I am obliged to be always upon my guard against him, and to exert my authority, which is not always sufficient to keep him within proper bounds.

The situation of the Governor of a distant Colony has, with the best aid that is possible for him to derive from his subordinate officers, enough of perplexity and vexation ; but when those who are sent expressly to assist him in the administration, become the principal sources of the embarrassments he meets with, it is hardly in human nature to support it with composure. On the opening of the session of the Legislature which hath just teminated, I received the most respectful and loyal addresses from both Houses in reference to the present posture of our affairs with the American States, and the representations of the dispositions of the Militia received from various parts of the Province are flattering. That their loyalty in general is to be relied on, I am ready to believe ; but unsupported by a competent military force, it would be too much to say that they are equal to defend the Province against the force that may be brought against it by the Americans. At present we have in all the different posts of the Province, on a frontier of more than five hundred miles, only the 41st Regiment, whose strength upon paper amounts only to ——, but whose efficient force, from the number of old and worn-out men, is in reality much less. This weakness of our military establishment has not escaped the notice of the Indian tribes who have been hitherto friendly to us, and my information from the agents of Government among them, as well as from other sources, leads me to believe that unless this establishment is very considerably augmented we must not rely on their co-operation in the event of a rupture with America.

Your friend Mr. Bond,* who is deservedly in no great repute in this country, and who has completely imposed on the Lords of the Committee of Trade and Plantations, not satisfied with

---

* This man, a hatter by trade, but too idle for his business, of character the very reverse of respectable, went to England in 1807 with some communication from Mr. Thorpe's Agricultural Society, and without any recommendation from the Governor procured an introduction to the Board of Trade, and under pretence of growing hemp, and extending the culture, by his example and instructions, cajoled them into an approval of his project, and through their recommendation obtained an order from Lord Castlereagh for 1,200 acres of land, one-half of which was to be cleared, and if the Governor had not any such in his gift he was to purchase it.

the 1,200 acres of land which I shall most certainly give him, agreeably to Lord Castlereagh's order, now applies to me for money about which His Lordship is silent, and which I certainly should not give to a better man than Mr. Bond without further authority for so doing.   He would be more likely to spend it in some other way than in the culture of hemp.   I would not, however, be surprised if the gentleman should in consequence complain of being thwarted and ill-used.   The culture of hemp is in a better train than Mr. Bond is likely to place it.   The Legislature have appropriated a sum of money to pay the growers of hemp in every part of the Province a liberal price for it on the spot, and through commissioners appointed for that purpose two considerable parcels have been consigned to Messrs. Brickwood & Daniels, in London, one in 1807 and another in 1808, and during the present year a larger and better sample will be shipped.

CHAPTER IX.

INCORPORATION OF KINGSTON—LETTER TO HIS EXCELLENCY FRANCIS
GORE—OBJECTS TO FEE FOR MILITIA COMMISSIONS—LETTER TO
MAJOR M'KENZIE—AMERICAN TROOPS ON THE FRONTIER—SHIP
OF WAR BUILDING AT OSWEGO—U. S. NAVAL OFFICERS IN KING-
STON HARBOUR.

IDEAS ON THE SUBJECT OF INCORPORATING THE TOWN OF
KINGSTON ARE SUBMITTED TO LIEUT.-GOVERNOR SIMCOE.

FIRST,—That the corporation should consist of a certain
number of persons, suppose four, to be increased in proportion
to the future population of the town, to be appointed by the
Governor, or elected by the inhabitants, or partly one and
partly the other, for the purpose of regulating the police of the
town under the following heads :

Regulations for preventing accidents by fire.

The times and places of holding the public markets.

Establishing the price and weight of bread.

Regulations for improving streets and keeping them clean.

Fares of carters within the limits.

Second. That the power of granting town lots should be vested in them, under the same instructions as were formerly laid
down for the Land Board, with a small fee for their clerk, who
is to be appointed by themselves.

Third. That a certain part of these lots, suppose one-sixth,
shall be reserved, and, together with the water lots and the
vacant ground beyond the limits of the town plot, and such as

may hereafter become vacant by the dereliction of Government, be vested in them, with power to lease or alienate the same reserving always a certain ground rent, and the money so raised to serve as a fund to be applied to the improvement of the town. That they should be empowered to purchase ground contiguous to the town, for the same purpose, if they should deem it expedient. That in the event of the town increasing beyond its present limits, their authority shall also extend over such addition, and include what is usually understood by the suburbs of a town. And it might also be expedient that they, or any three of them, should, six times in the year, hold Pleas of all causes under a certain sum, suppose £10, arising within their limits, to be tried by a jury, following, as nearly as circumstances will admit, the rules laid down for the proceedings in the District Court. I would not deem it expedient that this corporation should possess any power to prohibit any person whatever from exercising any lawful profession or calling within their limits, or to require any fee for the admission of any such persons.

To His Excellency Francis Gore.

KINGSTON, 18th April, 1808.

SIR,—The post some days ago, brought me a letter from the Adjutant General, enclosing the new Militia Law, and the schedule of fees intended to be charged on the commissions to be issued from your Excellency's office in consequence of it. As commissions in the Militia have heretofore been given free of expense, as well while we were a part of the late Province of Quebec as since we were made a separate Province, this measure, however trivial in itself, will give very general dissatisfaction, and be made the subject of much obloquy and misrepresentation.   Of the persons most concerned, some observe that however proper it might be that they should pay for a commission for any new appointment, yet for the mere renewal of the same commission under a different form they ought not to be put to any charge, and that if the Legislature have made this necessary, they ought to provide for the expense attending it.   Others say facetiously that they have no objection to the price of their commission being deducted from their first muster's subsistence.   That those who wish, at all events, to find fault with your Excellency's administration, will say worse of it, you will hardly doubt.   However disposed I may be to acquiesce in this or any other regulation you may deem expedient, I consider it as my duty, and what you will expect from me, to acquaint you with the public sentiment on the occasion.   What weight it ought to have is for your Excellency to judge.   As it has become necessary to form another company, this and the details required respecting the ages, &c., of the different officers will take up some time, and prevent me from replying at present to the Adjutant General.

It would seem that the Government at home deem the Militia of the Canadas of very considerable importance, from their sending out for them six inspecting field officers with the rank and pay of lieutenant-colonels.

To Major McKenzie.

KINGSTON, 2nd Nov., 1808.

SIR,—Some movements of troops and other transactions are taking place on the American frontier along the St. Lawrence and Lake Ontario, that ought not to escape observation. Within a few weeks more than 200 regular troops have been stationed between Great Sodus, about 20 miles to the westward of Oswego and Ogdensburg, of which there are two full companies at this latter place, which is at the head of the rapids, on the site of the old fort of Oswegatchie, and other troops are stated to be actually on their march to augment these several detachments to a thousand men.   Colonel Simmons, who is to command these troops, is said to have declared publicly that they would be augmented to 2,000 men before the spring.   He is an officer high in the confidence of the American Government, and is now actually examining the banks of the St. Lawrence for the most proper military stations.   The ostensible object of all this is, more completely to enforce the embargo ; but the vessel building at Oswego, which is to carry 18 guns, besides a 24-pounder in the bow, is much less adapted to this service than armed boats ; and it is now known that there were on board a small American schooner which put in here a few days ago, under pretence of being driven in by stress of weather, two officers of the American navy, who came for the express purpose of informing themselves of the different entrances to this port.   She came through the passage at the head of the Isle Tonté, and anchored in that neighbourhood a day or two. It is, in short, considered by some of the most intelligent men among whom these preparations are carrying on, that they proceed from views not altogether relating to the embargo, and at all events they appear to merit the notice of the Commander-in-Chief.

I am, &c.,

RICHARD CARTWRIGHT.

J